A Knight's Blood

Gwendolyn K. Blackthorne

Copyright © Gwendolyn K. Blackthorne 2022

First edition

Cover design by The Illustrated Page Book Design

Edited by Jay Eddy

eBook ISBN: 978-0-6456452-0-0

Paperback ISBN: 978-0-6456452-1-7

Published by BLOOD LUST PUBLISHING

To my dearest husband and beloved friends.

I couldn't have done this without you.

A Knight's Blood

1

There were very few times in Catherine's life where she felt truly untouchable; hearing the crowd cheering as she sat atop her steed, both clad in armour, was one of them.

Her chain mail shone in the sunlight, appearing almost luminescent white from certain angles. Golden filagree danced upon the edges of her helmet, which sat in her lap. The hem of her green and brown tabard fluttered around her thighs. Her family's crest, a stag standing either side of a portcullis, was emblazoned upon her chest and all over her horse's barding in white.

She waved at the crowd, her smile lighting up her face. Out of the corner of her eye, she could see her colleagues–now competitors–doing the same to stir up the audience. Interactions with the crowd were all part of the spectacle expected from a jousting tournament.

Despite the adrenaline that flowed through Catherine's veins, she couldn't banish the guilt that bubbled underneath. Her late mother's silver cross sat upon her chest underneath her shift, forever reminding her of the emptiness that came with grief. Never before had she felt it chill the flesh it rested upon, and yet, its growing cold coaxed goosebumps from her even in spring sunshine. She absentmindedly grasped for the cross but flinched when her gauntlet struck her mail instead. Her subconscious self-soothing habit had proven to be ineffective when wearing armour, but she still held her hand against the spot where her necklace laid against her chest. Though she couldn't feel the silver against her fingers and her palm, just the thought of the sensation calmed the guilt that undercut her brimming confidence.

The thump of someone's gloved hand against her knee pulled her away from thoughts of her mother.

Catherine looked down at the hand and found the kind, greying face of her former mentor, Sir Walter Alwyn looking up at her. Wrinkles formed in the corners of his eyes and mouth as his proud smile widened.

Walter held her prepared lance parallel to his body, the tip reaching up towards the sky. Though he was getting on in his years, he was still quite tall and stocky and retained a youthful spirit that made him a pleasure to be around. Walter no longer participated in tournaments. He attended the events anyway to support the greener knights and speak with those he hadn't seen in a while. His salt and pepper moustache twitched as he patted her knee again.

'Reaching for the necklace again, are we?' he teased. 'Hoping that it'll bring you good fortune today?'

While she appreciated her former mentor's humour, Catherine's smile waned. She let her hand fall from her tabard and rested it upon her helmet. Sorrow sat at the bottom of her throat where the cross hung, sending more chills through her body.

'Father didn't keep many of mother's belongings after she died. Her necklace is all I have,' Catherine replied.

He nodded in understanding, sympathetic to her grief. She needed someone to help guide her through the challenges of life and she thankfully had him and a few of her fellow knights to do so. But her father was not one of one of those guides.

9

Gwendolyn K. Blackthorne

Walter glanced over his shoulder at the crowd, watching how the nobles in the stands fawned over Lord Geoffrey Seymour–Catherine's father and lord of the village of Birkstead–up in the stands. The commonfolk gathered into groups at the barrier and cheered on their favourite knights while they prepared for the tournament ahead.

He returned his gaze back to Catherine, who put on a brave face after a moment of vulnerability and continued to interact with the crowd from afar.

A trio of trumpets sounded, drowning out the chattering from the audience and announcing that the event was about to begin. Once the final tone finished blaring, the only sounds that came from outside the jousting field were the whispers of nobles up on the stands as the announcer stepped up onto a platform close to the edge of the field. Dressed in the green and brown livery of House Seymour, the announcer clasped his hands together and grinned at the crowd as they waited with baited breath.

Both Catherine and Walter watched as he raised his hands to the heavens and drew in a deep breath. This was the moment the first bout would be announced. It was either a chance to scope out the competition before she faced them or go in almost blind. Either way, she was excited to prove to her father, and to herself, that she was worth more than who she could be married off to.

Catherine kept her expression light and airy, her posture relaxed, and her head held high. Her hands shook within her gauntlets, which, thankfully, wasn't noticeable. Her determination to impress and succeed weighed as heavily as her desire to keep her independence did.

'Welcome to the annual spring tournament! Because

our lord has been so generous, we have not only the knights of Birkstead, but warriors from all around England competing today!'

Catherine clenched her jaw as the nobles in the stands around her father went wild with applause.

'Unlike the other tournaments you've seen in the past, Lord Seymour's own daughter will be competing against her peers for your entertainment today. From seasoned knights to up-and-coming ones, we have an entertaining line-up.'

The crowd cheered and whooped as Catherine raised her hand above her head and waved at the sea of faces on the other side of the fence just as the other knights were. She couldn't help but to smile as pride swelled within her chest. Though she hated being paraded in front of nobles and knights like a prized cow, Catherine loved the thrill that came with donning her armour and crossing swords with opponents. Seeing the people scream and cheer for her and the rest of the knights made everything worth it. She wanted was to protect the people and show them that she cared for them, not sit in the manor and birth some nobleman's heir.

Her heart beat hard and fast against her ribs as she waited for the applause to die down so the announcer could reveal which match would be opening the tournament.

'For our first bout of the day, please welcome our favourite Sir Aldric Carey as he'll be facing off Lady Catherine Seymour in her jousting debut,' the announcer cried.

While the nobles up in the stands resigned themselves to a polite clap, the crowd shouted and threw their hands in the air with utter excitement.

Aldric grinned and threw his fist up into the air,

encouraging them to cheer louder.

They needed very little encouragement to do so, as they instantly responded with even more applause.

Aldric chuckled and slid his helmet into place, hiding his brown skin and his charming smile from the audience's view. Not even the act of covering his face curtailed the crowd's enthusiastic cheers. His squire handed him his shield and helped him adjust it until it sat just right.

Catherine's eyes widened.

She was up against one of her father's best jousters.

She glanced up at Geoffrey and bit back the urge to loudly damn him.

Her father relaxed into his throne and tilted his chin in the way that he usually did when he knew he was about to get his way.

A breath escaped through her nostrils as she glared at him, only just stopping the corner of her lip from quirking into a sneer at the last moment.

Catherine would prove him wrong.

'Don't let who you're competing against distract you. You know what to do,' Walter said, patting her knee reassuringly. 'Just remember: watch for an opening and guard yours as much as you can.'

Catherine pulled her gaze away from the stands and glanced down at her former mentor with a smile and a nod. 'You're right, thank you,' she replied.

She reached over and patted her grey horse's neck. 'We

know what to do, don't we, Smokey?'

Walter chuckled as he watched Smokey toss his head in response to his owner's question.

Steeling herself, Catherine drew in a breath and slid her helm over her head. She adjusted how she sat in her saddle and took her lance from Walter, who offered it up to her with an encouraging grin. He looked right and left to gauge how close the people around them were as he chose his words carefully.

Walter gave Smokey's neck a pat as he looked up at his former protégé, his voice a hushed whisper as he said, 'Don't overthink it; go with your gut. If you don't trust in God, trust in yourself. You know what to do. Knock him down, Cat.'

Before she could thank him, trumpets blared a three-toned tune that quietened the crowd down enough for the announcer to speak.

Both knights watched as the announcer raised his arm high above his head.

'Take your positions!'

'Good luck,' Walter called.

She urged Smokey to her end of the field and brought him to a halt. Her hands continued to tremble as she aimed her lance at her opponent's shield. Though she knew the bout would be over almost as soon as it started, the moments leading up to it stretched on forever.

Instead of picking apart Aldric's seemingly impenetrable form pre-joust, she adjusted her own to ensure that any weaknesses Walter had found during her training could not be exploited by Aldric.

13

'Begin!'

The crowd cheered louder as both Aldric and Catherine spurred their horses into a canter, barrelling down the field towards each other with their lances aimed at the other's shield.

The horses dug their hooves into the dirt, their steel shoes sending clumps of earth flying in all directions.

Catherine gritted her teeth. She fought against Smokey's movements to keep her lance steady. She slid into the slope of her saddle between every bound. Her blood pounded against her ears. Sounds blurred and fell into the background. Her heartbeat drowned out everything around her.

Aldric and his horse quickly bounded towards her, his lance fast approaching.

Their lances clashed against each other's shields, splintering into thousands of little shards.

Catherine pushed her weight into her shield and gritted her teeth as she fought to keep herself seated. The impact of the lance upon her shield threatened to push her out of her saddle. Sharp pain shot down her forearm.

A chorus of gasps fell over the field like the wooden pieces that scattered over the dirt. The crowd leant forward in awe as they watched one of the knights fall, grimacing as the sound of metal colliding with the ground rang through the air.

And as quickly as it started, it was all over.

Catherine winced, but shifted her weight to keep herself from toppling off Smokey's saddle. She pulled on the reigns, forcing him to slow down. She turned Smokey around once she reached the other end of the field and saw his young squire help Aldric to his feet. Her mouth hung open as the outcome of her very first joust dawned on her.

She'd won.

The silence from the crowd wafted over the field like a bad smell as Aldric got to his feet with the help of his squire. The unnerving quiet was shattered by the booming sound of the other knight's raucous laughter. It only got louder as he pulled his helmet off and tucked it under his arm, glee apparent upon his face.

After clearing his throat, the announcer raised his hands above his head and turned to gaze upon the crowd.

'Lady Seymour wins!'

Moments after she was declared the victor, the audience clapped and cheered as if she had become their new favourite competitor. Some even shouted her name.

Though she couldn't pick out individual faces, the excitement emanating from the crowd was utterly contagious. It crashed over her like a wave and served to swell the exhilaration that already coursed through her. Her back straightened and she held her head up high, smiling with pride.

Aldric patted the squire on the back and stumbled towards Catherine, grinning as if he were teaching his own daughter how to ride a horse. He patted Smokey's neck and smiled up at Catherine as she removed her helmet as well.

'Well, well… Look at you. All grown up and beating me in a joust. Sir Alwyn may not be competing anymore, but it seems as if he still the master of the chivalrous arts,' he commented.

Catherine brushed a dark stray hair back behind her ear

and smirked. Though pride was one of the seven deadly sins, she couldn't deny that it felt good. It felt powerful. For religious leaders that thought themselves to be so pious yet self-serving, she could see why they would preach pride's vile potential to a group they viewed as lesser. There was power in pride. She was going to keep as much of her own power as possible.

'It was an honour to be tutored by Sir Alwyn, just as it was to joust you, Sir Carey. In the end, the outcome of this sport is partially governed by practice and partially by chance,' Catherine replied.

Aldric snorted in agreement. 'Aye, that it is. When you get off your horse, how about you join my wife and I in our tent? Sabina wishes to indulge in court gossip with someone she can trust to give her the unembellished truth.'

Catherine suppressed a chuckle and smiled wider.

Like herself, Lady Carey found interacting with other nobles tedious and a complicated dance of social manipulation that served no real purpose. While Sabina wasn't a knight or trained in the ways of combat like Catherine was, it was refreshing to have someone around who wasn't constantly trying to get into her father's good books.

'I will have to leave every now and again to prepare for upcoming matches, but I would be delighted,' Catherine replied.

'Wonderful. Please invite Walter over too. We have that wine from France he likes so much,' Aldric said before he wandered off to his tent, following his squire as the boy led his horse to the hitching post outside.

2

Walter and Aldric sat outside, debating who would win each match as the competition continued throughout the day.

Sabina stepped out of the tent, only glancing back to share an unamused roll of her eyes with Catherine as she followed a group of noblewomen towards the stands to discuss the next feast.

Catherine's chest shook with silent laughter and she shrugged at Sabina before the noblewoman had to leave. The smile that Catherine wore fell and was replaced by the shadow of a frown. Her gauntlet hit her tabard and the chain mail underneath with a dull thump and she sighed, remembering that the necklace she often caressed in times of loneliness and stress was underneath her armour. Her wrists rested against her thighs, weighed down by her gauntlets. She got up from the stool and wandered outside the tent to see what the other two knights were up to.

Aldric glanced over his shoulder when he heard the tent flap move and waved Catherine over to where he and Walter were spectating with goblets full of that French wine Walter liked.

Without hesitation, Catherine headed over towards them and pulled a spare stool with her to sit close so they didn't have to talk any louder than they needed to. She didn't want anyone to hear something that could be used against her to gain favour

17

with her father. Though she trusted both Aldric and Walter with her life, there were quite a few of their peers that she didn't.

'It's about time you joined us,' Walter said. 'Your father will likely expect you to have seen some of the men he's invited. He's pushing for you to pick a husband soon.'

'Surely, he knows his attempts to marry me off are futile. I don't need a man who will ask me to hang up my sword because he's expected to be the protector and I'm not. I can tell you now; there is no man here I would consider marrying,' Catherine stated.

Aldric straightened his shoulders and glanced at the older knight with a mixture of surprise and concern. His forehead creased as his brows furrowed. He opened his mouth and closed it as he attempted to find the words.

Though she was his liege's daughter, he still saw her as the second daughter that he and Sabina never had. He loved having her around as it gave his child hope that she wasn't stuck doing what the court deemed as acceptable and nothing more.

'You may change your mind in the future,' Aldric said with a joking shrug of his shoulders.

'Cat? Change her mind? She's as stubborn as an unbroken stallion,' Walter commented with a scoff. The old knight reached over and brushed some of Catherine's stray dark hairs behind her ear. His skin crinkled the corners of his lips as he gave her a fond smile. 'But, if they cannot see the beauty in her stubbornness, they don't deserve her.'

She quirked an eyebrow at her former mentor. A wonky, unsure smile graced her face. 'Thanks?'

Before Aldric got the chance to speak, the announcer

raised his hands up to the sky and the trumpets rung out in their usual triple tones to get the crowd's attention.

All three knights turned towards the announcer, waiting in anticipation to see who would participate in the next bout.

'For the final qualifying round, we will be seeing Sir Robert Badden joust the warrior known only as the Crusader. Please give it up for our competitors as they take their places.'

The crowd cheered as both knights steered their horses towards their respective ends of the field. Robert waved and smiled at a trio of maidens who stood close to the field boundary, causing them to giggle amongst themselves. Once their giggle fit ran its course, they gave him their flirtiest smiles.

Robert turned his head towards where Catherine sat with Aldric and Walter, giving her his best grin with a tilt of his chin.

Catherine didn't notice Robert at all.

Cold prickled the skin around her mother's cross as she watched the Crusader ride past on a horse with a coat as dark as night. Ignoring the tingling sensation underneath her mother's cross, she analysed the knight's plain black tabard for any coat of arms or identifiers but found nothing. She narrowed her eyes and sat up straighter as the sun reflected off the unknown knight's helmet, proving that it was indeed as dark as their horse's mane. Curiosity got the better of her as she wondered which talented smith had figured out how to make their steel as dark as death's embrace.

No matter how hard she tried, she couldn't tear her gaze away from the knight in the shadowy armour.

'Have you ever heard of this "Crusader" before?'

Catherine asked the other two knights.

'No, my lady,' Aldric replied, barely stopping a smile from touching his lips.

Walter simply shook his head in reply.

Catherine noticed Aldric's squire waddling towards the newcomer with their lance swaying dangerously above him, ready to fall on top of him at any second. The doe-eyed, thoughtless smile that curled upon his lips showed that he wouldn't care if the lance flattened him; he only wished to serve the Crusader in order to garner their continued attention.

'Your lance,' he announced and held the lance out for the Crusader to take from his unsteady hands.

She ran her hand through her hair, pulling pieces from her already messy braid onto her face. Watching the Crusader pat the squire on his head sent shivers running down Catherine's whole body.

Walter saw his former student tremble and clutch her arms as if she were sitting in front of a fire in a snowstorm.

'Are you feeling alright?' he asked, placing a hand upon her shoulder.

'Oh yes, quite well,' she answered. She glanced down at the ground and then up at the Crusader again. Her chest tingled as freezing tendrils slithered their way down her torso from where the cross sat against her flesh. 'Just cold.'

Begin!'

Every onlooker watched the match intensely as the horses bounded towards each other without slowing. Both horses snorted every time their front hooves struck the ground. The lances quickly closed the distance between the two competitors, stealing precious seconds for any adjustments that would keep them on their horses. Their lances crashed against their shields, splintering with an almighty crack that rivalled thunder.

The maidens who flirted with Robert prior to his bout screeched and clasped their chests.

The object of their affections fell from his horse, landing on the ground with a metallic clang that made many of the spectators's skin crawl.

The Crusader brought their horse to a halt at the other end of the field, ignoring the crowd's open mouths as they tried to decide whether to cheer or gasp at the newcomer's victory.

It wasn't long before the announcer proclaimed the dark knight the victor of the bout and the audience cheered for the winner as they did everyone else.

She pulled her gaze away from the Crusader and watched her father's expression darken as he stared at Robert. Anger coated her thoughts scarlet as she watched a sneer touch Geoffrey's face whilst he watched the knight clamber to his feet. She knew what disappointment looked like upon her father's face. She had a bad feeling that the knight he favoured as his next up-and-coming champion would receive a vicious tongue lashing for his performance. Catherine's bad feeling fled as soon as she realised it was one less tongue lashing directed at her.

Catherine's body stopped trembling when the Crusader reached the other side of the field. Her necklace ceased to prickle her flesh with phantom cold. Upon noticing this change, Catherine pursed her lips and stared at the Crusader through narrowed eyes. She tried her best to keep her curiosity to herself, but the way her brow furrowed as her mind raced gave her away.

'Something on your mind?' Walter asked.

'This Crusader is quite skilled for a newcomer. It's going to be interesting to see how far they get,' Catherine replied.

Aldric looked at her, barely hiding his amused smirk. 'England is much bigger than just Birkstead, Catherine. In fact, there's a whole world out there beyond our shores. Just because this "Crusader" isn't known here, doesn't mean they're not as skilled as anyone else here.'

'You've made your point,' Catherine said, rolling her eyes.

Her squire attempted to get her attention from across the field, but Catherine couldn't pull her gaze away from the warrior upon the dark horse.

Walter quizzically narrowed his eyes at Catherine.

'Cat?'

She blinked quickly and shook her head at the sound of her name. Catherine drew in a deep breath, unwilling to draw attention to the blush that warmed her cheeks and faced Walter with a smile. Her gauntlets clunked against each other as she laid one on top of the other upon her thigh.

'Yes?' Catherine asked in reply.

'We should return to your tent. I believe the second round of bouts will be starting soon and you should start preparing,' Walter suggested.

'Very well. Thank you for entertaining us during the last

few matches, Aldric,' Catherine said as she got to her feet and gave the other knight a small nod.

Aldric smiled widely and nodded to Catherine in return. 'It was my pleasure. I look forward to seeing how far you go in the tournament.'

'As do I,' Catherine said with an unsure sigh.

Walter beckoned to her and playfully huffed with impatience.

Catherine followed him across the field.

Her chest tightened and her body shivered. She looked over at the Crusader and, for a fleeting moment, swore that she'd seen two shining red orbs in the darkness behind the helmet's visor. Before she could look again, the Crusader's head had turned.

Catherine's curiosity continued to run rampant as she followed Walter into her tent to prepare for her next match.

3

Bouts came and went as the sun moved across the almost cloudless sky. The outcome of each match was followed by cheers from the excitable crowd. Such joy was followed by gossip from nobles speculating who was most likely to win the tournament.

For everyone but his daughter and the Crusader, to win the tournament was to guarantee Geoffrey's benevolence. And his benevolence came with the chance to be considered for the coveted role as the next Lord of Birkstead by making his daughter their bride.

Catherine hadn't been unhorsed yet, but that didn't mean she was unharmed. Spots on her arms were so tender that she was sure they would blossom into bright purple bruises before the day was out. Exhaustion dragged her closer towards the earth, weighing her down until she felt as if she were thrown into a lake in her armour, sinking below the surface, knowing any attempt to swim would be futile.

She dabbed the sweat from her brow with a towel, scowling as strands of wet hair stuck to her forehead. Her jaw clicked as she wiggled it back and forth, dispersing the pain from clenching her teeth too often.

Despite being unheard of before this tournament, the Crusader won every bout they competed in with ease.

Catherine watched every match the Crusader

participated in, almost snarling at how effortlessly the warrior performed. When an opposing lance struck their shield, the Crusader barely flinched or even shifted from the force of the impact. The Crusader sat tall upon their horse and faced the slowly setting sun with their broken lance pointed straight up toward the sky.

Catherine threw her towel on the ground and picked up her helmet, placing it on her saddle horn before she swung up onto Smokey for the final time today. She slid her helmet over her head and looked down at her former mentor.

Walter held her shield, looking at her with pride. Years of persistence and training had paid off, and he felt more like a father encouraging his daughter instead of a teacher assisting his student prepare for her last match of the day; the bout that would decide the victor of the tournament.

'Don't be hard on yourself if the bout doesn't end in your favour, Cat. You've already far exceeded your father's expectations of you and proven yourself more capable than anyone he invited specifically to compete against you,' Walter said, handing her the shield.

Though he couldn't see it, a tight-lipped smile stretched across her lips as she picked up the shield and adjusted her grip. Whether what her former mentor said about her father was true or not, she still wanted to prove to him that she was worth more than being someone's key to Birkstead.

'It's just you and the Crusader now. You've beaten every knight your father has invited to his tournament. Take a deep breath and try to relax. You'll do well; I know you will.'

Catherine rolled her shoulders and sat up as straight as she could in the saddle, leaning into the slope to centre herself. She tried her best not to look down at Walter, for she knew that if she did, she'd want to throw herself into his arms and hug him tight. Catherine found his belief in her both endearing and touching to the point that if she dwelled on it long enough, she'd cry.

'Thank you for being there for me,' she said, her voice shaky.

Walter's smile softened. He reached up to pat her knee the same way he did when she was eight and just starting her journey towards knighthood. Pride glassed over his eyes and his cheeks trembled trying to keep his smile wide. Wrinkles bunched up on his hand and in the corners of his eyes. The older knight looked so vulnerable, so fragile.

'You were my student for years. What kind of teacher would I be if I didn't support you after you were knighted?' he asked.

She went to respond, but was cut off by the announcer proclaiming that the final bout would be between Catherine and the warrior known as the Crusader.

The crowd cheered as the dark warrior veered their horse towards their end of the field.

It was time to see which of the two would be left upon their horse at the other end of the jousting field.

Walter handed Catherine her lance.

She took it and held it firmly without saying a word.

The older knight clasped his hands in front of him and stepped back to let her urge her steed up to her end of the field. His pride in Catherine stood strong against the worry threatening to corrode it.

She kept her head held high as she tugged on the reigns

and Smokey came to a halt at her starting position. Catherine clenched her jaw and focused her gaze on the dark armoured warrior on the other side of the field. Her heart thumped hard against her chain mail as she waited for the announcer to give the cue to begin.

Birkstead was her family's town; there was no way she'd allow herself to be struck off her horse on the very ground she called home.

Catherine sat deep in her saddle and tightened her grip on her shield, waiting for what felt like an eternity for the announcer's call.

'Begin!'

She urged her stallion into a gallop as she lowered her lance, aiming it at the Crusader's shield as they sped down the field. The pounding of Smokey's hooves against the earth matched the pace of the blood pounding against her eardrums.

As she got closer to the Crusader, her flesh began to shiver as if she'd fallen naked into snow. The skin around her necklace prickled underneath the silver, prodding her chest with thousands of tiny needles.

Catherine clenched her jaw harder to force her body to cooperate. Her lance deviated from the direction she wanted it to point in slowly. She grunted in frustration as she wrestled to reposition it.

The urge to close her eyes rushed over her as she sped closer to the warrior coming at her from the opposite direction. She refused to give in. She was mere seconds away from seeing whether or not she would become the victor of her father's tournament. There was no way she was going to deny herself the satisfaction of realising she was triumphant.

Both lances splintered as they struck metal, the cracking of wood splitting the air like thunder.

A chorus of gasps followed and fled into the breeze, dropping another blanket of tense silence over the spectators.

What little air that filled Catherine's lungs was stolen by the Crusader's lance as it shattered against her shield. The impact forced her to drop her broken lance. The weight of her mail and shield dragged her out of her saddle.

Catherine hit the ground hard.

Pain tore through her back and constricted her chest further, working in tandem with her necklace's chill to hold her captive upon the dirt.

She stared up at the purple and orange that tinged the darkening blue sky above her.

The announcer named the Crusader as the winner of the tournament.

The crowd cheered.

Lord Geoffrey Seymour sat in a chair fashioned like a throne, slowly clapping with an expression as dark as a brewing storm.

Catherine could barely make out any words from the sea of voices that washed over her. She lay on her back, gasping for air so her lungs no longer burned.

Everything ached.

The biting cold that grasped her flesh began to seep out of her bones and into the earth underneath her. Tears of fury and shame prickled the corners of her eyes. Her wrists ached as she balled her hands into fists.

She'd lost the bout.

Not only that, she lost the bout on her family's land, with her father watching from the stands.

Geoffrey would hold this loss over her until the day either of them died.

The Crusader remained seemingly unfazed by the impact of Catherine's lance, just as they had with the bouts before. Their tabard bore new gashes and exposed the chain mail underneath. They thrust their broken lance in the air, igniting another, louder, wave of cheers from the audience.

Walter ran to Catherine's side, skidding through the dirt on his knees to stop beside her. Panic aged him more than the passing of time as he ripped off her helmet. He let a heavy sigh of relief fall from his lips as he saw Catherine's eyes move to look at him.

She continued to gasp like a fish pulled from water, forcing as much air into her aching lungs as she possibly could.

Relief relaxed his shoulders and they drooped back down. After centring himself, he sat back on his heels and ran his hand across Catherine's cheek.

'Are you alright?' he asked.

No matter how angry she was, her pained expression softened and her fists opened out. The worry and panic on Walter's face made her chest throb with guilt as well as pain. She found the strength to nod.

'Sore,' she groaned.

'I bet you would be; that was a nasty fall,' Walter replied. 'Do you think you can get up?'

'I believe so. I'll need some help getting to my feet,' she said.

The old knight slid his arm behind her neck and held her hand, frowning as she winced. He gently pulled her up and stopped when she was sitting upright. He held Catherine steady as she swayed back and forth.

Catherine hissed and bit back tears as her chain mail pressed against on her tender flesh. She was sure there would be bruises up her body bigger than her shield come morning. Catherine opened her eyes once the aching subsided slightly. The earth no longer swayed underneath her.

She saw the Crusader slip into a bright red and yellow tent on the other side of the field.

'I'm proud of you, you know,' Walter whispered, not wanting those who began to crowd around the two of them to hear.

His hushed tones weren't for his sake, but Catherine's. He knew she was proud, overly headstrong, and stubborn. The fact that she'd been defeated would've been devastating enough, she didn't want to give anyone any more ammunition to use against her.

'I want to get out of this armour,' she pleaded as tears of pain fell down her ruddy cheeks.

Walter helped her to her feet, draping one of her arms over his shoulders and supporting her with his other arm. Her pained whimpers broke his heart. He led her towards her tent. Seeing the tears welling in the corners of her eyes, he knew that she needed to be away from prying eyes before she would let her emotions break free.

Gwendolyn K. Blackthorne

4

Dressed in a forest green surcoat and brown leather boots that covered every inch of her battered and bruised body, Catherine walked across the field towards the Crusader's tent as gracefully as she could without further aggravating her injuries.

Despite Walter's pleas for her to rest, Catherine wanted to look the warrior who'd bested her in the eye.

She ignored the aches and pains that plagued her body with every step. Aware of the eyes that stared at her, Catherine kept her movements smooth and her chin held high; any sign of weakness would give onlookers the smallest reason to discredit all of her accomplishments. It was more than likely her loss would prompt them to do so already, so she refused to give them anything else to talk about. As long as her lungs breathed air, she'd fight to maintain her reputation as a knight and the little freedoms that came along with it.

The closer she got to the tent, the more her chest prickled from the growing chill that clung to her mother's cross. No matter how curious she was about the sudden onset of frost that gripped her body whenever she got close to the Crusader, Catherine kept her composure. Her flesh shivered and goosebumps rose underneath her surcoat but she did her best to ignore it. Pain nor cold would get the better of her.

Without announcing herself or even asking Aldric's

squire with the eerily blank stare to do so, Catherine swept the flap aside and sauntered into the tent. Catherine winced and finally grasped the pendant with her fingers, pulling it out from underneath her surcoat and dropping the cross against the fabric so it would not distract her from satiating her curiosity.

She continued forward until she found someone sitting on a chair with their back to her.

Catherine stopped and tilted her head to the side. Her mouth opened slightly as she stood mesmerised by the way the shadows danced upon hair that looked like polished copper. A pale hand reached over their head and slid their long, pointed nails through their hair. They shook the strands to detangle some of the knots that formed at the base of their neck.

A shiver ran up Catherine's spine as she wondered if this person was indeed the warrior who unhorsed her and the rest of the knights they came up against. Her breath caught in her throat as she caught a glimpse of their lilac-tinged lips before they moved out of her sight. White cotton fabric floated around their body, obscuring their form in the same way that some of Catherine's own shifts would have. Catherine's heart almost stopped when she saw the Crusader's face.

'Ah, Lady Seymour,' a feminine voice crooned, an Irish accent thick upon her tongue. The figure in the chair turned around and crossed one leg over the other, draping her arm over the back of the chair. The corners of her lips stretched into a smile that exhibited a pair of incisors sharper than the tip of a dagger. 'I'm glad to see you up and about after that nasty fall. I hoped you weren't severely injured; it would be a shame to have such talent go to waste.'

Catherine's cheeks heated. She kept her hands behind

33

her back, wringing them nervously so the Crusader couldn't see. Panic swirled within her stomach as she realised that she had come to find that the warrior who bested her had stolen her breath more than once that day.

'I am glad as well. I believe I was luckier than others. The most I'll have is a few bruises. Though your compliments are kind, I cannot ignore the fact that you're also a talented jouster and horsewoman,' Catherine replied, pronouncing her words slowly to not trip over her tongue. 'It seems as if you know who I am, but I do not even know your name. May I have the pleasure of knowing the name that the Crusader prefers to go by outside of the jousting field?'

The Crusader's copper hair shone as if she had strands of pure gold woven into it when she turned her head a little more towards Catherine. Her smile returned to her lips as her gaze drank in what was visible of Catherine's figure. The Crusader hummed with approval.

'Helena.'

The longer Catherine gazed at Helena, the faster her heart raced. Blush crept up to her cheeks yet again, colouring her face a deep shade of pink. Even after letting out a small breath to steady herself, the knight's insides twisted and threatened to liquify there and then. Her skin prickled from the icy aura that clung to her mother's necklace as the chill seeped through her surcoat and caressed her flesh once more.

In all her years, she'd never felt this way over any man, especially one who'd attempted to win her affections. And yet, Helena had reduced her to a quivering mess that struggled to properly enunciate without twisting her own tongue. Was this what the maidens who fawned over knights felt when they were acknowledged by them? Was this what attraction felt like? The awkward helplessness that gripped her speeding heart only served to frustrate Catherine more. So many questions cluttered her thoughts so much that she was sure she appeared as devoid of thought as the squire outside.

Catherine cleared her throat and returned her thoughts to the current moment. She shifted on her feet and lowered her gaze for a moment, regaining some sense of her cool façade before lifting her chin back up and making contact with Helena's haunting crimson eyes.

'It's not often that I meet another woman gifted in the art of battle,' Catherine said.

Helena's shift tumbled down over her pale knees as she stood up from her chair and ran her fingers through her hair again. Her lips parted in an amused smile, flashing her unnaturally white, sharp teeth at Catherine. Her bare feet brushed the worn rug that was laid over the dirt as she took slow, measured steps towards Catherine.

Despite the fact that she took as many hard hits as Catherine did, not a single spot on her skin was blemished by blossoming bruises. Sure, she had the odd freckle here and there, but she appeared as if she'd sat up in the stands the whole time.

Catherine's breath twirled in the air between her and Helena in a thin mist before it disappeared into nothingness.

'That may be so, but that doesn't change the fact that women like us can take advantage of men believing we're nothing more than pawns,' Helena said, pausing as she stopped before Catherine. There was barely more than a dagger's length between them. The Crusader lowered her gaze and stared at the side of Catherine's neck before she looked into Catherine's eyes. 'They don't expect us to best them at their own game.'

'Indeed,' Catherine replied, unsure of what else she could add to the conversation.

She was entranced by the way in which Helena's crimson irises shifted in the light. It reminded her of how sunshine hit fresh blood on a tilting blade's surface.

While Catherine had briefly noticed beautiful women before, she had never been so tongue-tied and starry-eyed over one before. The closer she looked at Helena's arms, the more she noticed raised scars so pale they blended into her skin as if they were never there. They appeared long since healed, but remained as reminders of battles she both won and lost.

Helena's face was close enough that Catherine could've felt her breath brush her face, and yet, she didn't exhale anything at all.

Catherine's breath, however, remained unusually foggy; flowing freely from her chapped lips.

The Crusader's lips parted as she went to speak. Her pale finger reached out and touched the cross upon Catherine's chest. Before she could get any words out, she hissed and retracted her finger from the cross the moment she touched it. She wrapped her hand around the finger, her beautiful face contorted in pain.

The mental fog that obscured everything but Helena's beauty and melodious voice evaporated from Catherine's mind the moment Helena scowled like a wounded predator.

Catherine's heart pounded faster than rain on the Seymour manor's roof during a storm. Though the butterflies in her stomach didn't settle, she was speechless over Helena for another reason.

Fear crawled its way up her spine, digging its claws into

her vertebrae as it moved higher and higher. Anger chased after fear, gaining ground in an attempt to squash her fear and shame.

Her dominant hand slid down to her sword, resting upon the hilt lazily as she'd seen many other knights do. Catherine loosely wrapped her fingers around the hilt, just in case she needed to leap into action for her own preservation.

'Are you alright?' Catherine asked, dread coursing through her body.

Helena nodded and lowered her hands as she forced a smile onto her lips. 'I'm very allergic to some metals, that's all. Is that silver by any chance?'

'Yes, it was my mother's. It was given to her by an archivist when she visited the Holy See,' Catherine answered.

Helena smiled meekly and let out a small laugh to hide the uncertainty cracking through her façade. 'Ah, that's why. My skin is very sensitive to silver.'

Catherine grasped the cross with her other hand and grimaced as the freezing silver prickled her fingers.

'I've never seen anyone react like that to any metal before,' Catherine remarked.

Helena laughed, dismissing Catherine's comment by smirking. 'Then you haven't seen a severe allergy before. I wouldn't expect you to have seen one before now; knights tend to have an enviable constitution.'

It wasn't until those words left her mouth did the pieces finally fall into place.

The majority of Helena's features matched that of the

undead she'd been trained to protect the people from. The creatures that slunk in villages and cities during the night and drained sleeping peasants of their blood in the safety of their own homes. The same creatures that used their unassuming exterior to lure the naïve to their doom. There was no denying it, especially after how well the Crusader performed in the tournament.

It suddenly dawned on her why her mother's silver necklace grew cold around Helena and no one else.

The cross helped her sense the presence of undead.

Helena was a vampire.

Catherine took a deep breath and clenched her jaw as she forced the corner of her lips to quirk into a small smile. She tightened her grip on her sword and stared into Helena's crimson eyes, grounding herself by reminding herself that the reason they had that ethereal glow was that Helena wasn't human. Not anymore.

'Of course. I forget myself. Congratulations on winning the tournament. You were truly the best warrior of the day,' Catherine said and gave a small bow from her waist.

Helena smiled back at the knight and bowed her head in return. 'I found you equally worthy, Lady Seymour.'

Without uttering another word, Catherine turned around and let her false smile fall.

Despite the fact that she knew the woman was a vampire, fighting Helena one on one, even if she was unarmed, was a death sentence. If she attempted to take her on in battle, she'd need at least two other knights by her side to balance out the sheer speed and strength that vampires like Helena possessed.

But first, she needed to meet with her lord father before

she even thought about bringing this up with Walter and Aldric. And her father despised being kept waiting.

5

Lord Geoffrey invited nobles and knights alike into his manor for his famous post-tournament feast. He wished to speak to his only child before they joined the social affair he'd orchestrated. Geoffrey had to ensure that she behaved herself in front of his colleagues.

Since leaving the field, she had to make herself presentable to her father's guests, even if she was covered in bruises from head to toe. The green hemline of Catherine's kirtle swished against the ground as she walked into her father's study without knocking, her head held high and her fists gripping the fabric as if it were his neck. Not wanting to go without some indication of her standing as a knight, she kept the silver dagger she received after she'd taken her vow strapped to her belt. It wasn't as comfortable to wield as a sword and shield, but she'd rather have it than no weapon at all.

There was, after all, a vampire hiding in Birkstead.

Lord Seymour stared up at his daughter, his squared jaw tensed and his lips pursed. He put his quill down and threaded his fingers together as he leant against the desk with his elbows.

Geoffrey sported a beard that looked almost as greasy as what was left of his balding hair. He adjusted the velvet plumed hat on top of his head so that it still appeared as if he had as much hair as he did when he married Catherine's mother.

Despite the fact that his daughter had arrived as

requested, she refused to show the decorum expected of a young noblewoman. He'd ensured she could appear as if she belonged, but he doubted she could ever seamlessly blend into a crowd of nobles.

'I thought I raised you with more manners,' he remarked, his frown pulling the lines on his face downward.

Catherine tilted her head to the side and smirked ever so slightly.

'You would've had to raise me yourself to do that, now wouldn't you?' she questioned. She let the smirk fall as she quirked an eyebrow, daring him to correct her.

The intensity of his glare would've made any other noble quiver. The way his bushy eyebrows framed his eyes made his glare all the more dangerous. It was the same expression he employed when his underlings proved incapable of following directions. He sucked in a breath and straightened up even more to appear bigger than he was. Geoffrey's glare darkened as his building ire tugged his lips into a sneer.

Though Catherine was a noblewoman by birth, she had completed the years of gruelling training needed to have the chance to be ordained a knight. She came lance to lance with a vampire and somehow walked away alive. Catherine knew that she was worth more than her father deemed. She refused to bow to his silent attempt to dominate her and tilted her chin upward, forcing the shadows that rested upon her brow to slide down to her soft cheekbones. His current tactics proved effective in her childhood, but Catherine was a grown woman facing challenges that scared her more than her father's anger ever did and ever could again.

She let go of her skirts and let the crinkled fabric fall

41

Gwendolyn K. Blackthorne

down to the floor. Catherine clasped her hands together and walked over to her father's desk, ignoring the fact that she had very little power to advocate for herself and her wants. She realised that she had to be the one to break the silence.

'What did you wish to speak to me about, my lord?' Catherine asked.

Geoffrey glanced down at the letter he was in the middle of writing and returned his gaze to his child, disappointed she remained stronger than he hoped she was.

'Though your insolence is infuriating, I'm glad you came quickly. We have to discuss the outcome of the tournament today,' Geoffrey announced, lacing his fingers together.

'Am I correct in the assumption that you wish to marry me off to one of the knights that took part today? The ones that I bested?' Catherine questioned, knowing that the answer was yes.

Lord Geoffrey ran his tongue across his teeth, feeling the chipped edges of his teeth prickle in their wake. 'While the Crusader was the victor, I do not wish to marry my only daughter off to a warrior no one has heard of until today. You cannot carry on the family name into marriage, so I will ensure that you are paired with a reputable noble or knight in order to keep Birkstead in capable and worthy hands.'

Her hand lazily trailed down her dress and wrapped around her dagger's hilt as she frowned. The bridge of her nose crinkled.

Staying quiet was the best way to deal with her father. Anger slithered down the back of her neck like a snake ready to strike, grabbing hold of her flesh and sending shivers across her pained shoulders.

A Knight's Blood

Her father was no man she would call capable and worthy of overseeing the village that their family had presided over for more than a century.

He slouched in his chair, distracted by the gems that clung to fingers that had never seen a day of manual labour. The only show of piety she'd seen from Geoffrey was the sheer amount of money he paid the Church in Indulgences to ensure there was a place in Heaven for him. The very fact that he'd rather spend Birkstead's taxes on entertaining other nobles than doing anything that would benefit the people annoyed Catherine to no end.

'It seems a little unfair to ask that from a future son-in-law when you can barely meet those standards yourself, wouldn't you agree?' Catherine asked, her voice low and wrathful.

The nobleman got up from his chair and adjusted the string of golden squares set with various precious stones around his neck. Geoffrey cleared his throat and walked out from behind his desk, taking slow, small steps. He kept his gaze trained on his daughter as he moved around the room, mimicking the way a wolf circled a rival before launching, teeth bared.

'You should hold your tongue on matters you don't understand,' Geoffrey announced.

Catherine met his gaze with the same ferocity she would give an enemy on the battlefield. She pursed her lips, not certain that her father had his priorities in the right place. Catherine allowed herself another second to dwell on that thought. The realisation he was always like that trickled into the forefront of her mind. She only noticed because it was just more obvious now.

Hand on her dagger's hilt, she adjusted how she stood, adopting more of a battle stance. She was used to fighting for

what she wanted out of life and she'd be damned if she let someone else continue to dictate how she lived.

'While I am aware that I do not have a say in who I
marry and when that occurs, I will be heard on other matters
regarding my future. I understand that you have to do what you
must for the people, but I would've thought that you would have
some interest in my happiness as well as theirs,' Catherine spat
in reply. 'I have been proven wrong by you before, but there are
matters of your character that are always proven right. Just like
the people you claim to protect: I'm nothing but a pawn to you.
Everyone, even mother, end up being pieces in your game for
power. You care about no one but yourself.'

'Enough!'

Geoffrey's nostrils flared as he slammed his hands on his
desk. He puffed out his chest and looked down on his daughter,
ensuring that she remembered her place. His expression was
darker than a storm and his face flushed red.

Nothing angered him more than when his only daughter
decided to be stubborn. If he squinted enough, she was the spit-
ting image of her mother in both appearance and temperament.
Geoffrey had no say in his own marriage, and yet Agnes became
the one part of his life he didn't regret. Catherine, however, he
did regret from time to time. This was one of those times.

'You spent so much time training to be a knight that
you have no idea how to converse with those at your station and
above without behaving like a barbarian. I have to take control,
otherwise you'll ruin our name even more than you already
have,' Geoffrey chided.

Catherine scoffed and shook her head. 'My martial training is not to blame. The family name has been soiled by your

ego and insatiable lust for luxury.'

Geoffrey's face reddened. His hands balled into fists by his side, his nose scrunching at his only child. 'I've done everything that's been expected of me in my lifetime, same with your mother. She took on her role with a grace and kindness that could rival many saints. The Church wouldn't have the ability to teach monster-hunting techniques to knights like you without her.'

'Mother's achievements are hers and hers alone. What have you done to be so high and mighty about doing what's expected of you?' Catherine asked.

'I gave her the time and resources she needed to continue her research in peace,' Geoffrey replied. 'I protected her as best as I could from those who wished to hinder her progress.'

She glared at her father, biting back the urge to unsheathe her weapon and press its edge against his neck. The rage she'd pushed down time and time again bubbled up from the darkest corners of her mind. It was just like him to want the most fanfare for doing the easiest of tasks and it irritated her to no end.

She ran her tongue over her teeth and shook her head once more. 'You're pathetic.'

'Catherine-'

The knight didn't let her father finish his sentence. She finally spoke the bitter thoughts that lingered in her mind every time he brought up her duty to marry.

'If you're that desperate to pass on the family legacy without recognising your own selfishness, marry again and have a son. That way, Birkstead can stay connected to your name and your bloodline.'

'That's enough,' Geoffrey warned.

She refused to listen. 'We both know Birkstead would go to an unmarried son without problem. You don't pursue that because you know that no one would willingly marry you, no matter how much you offered them.'

'Enough!'

Before she could argue back, he shoved his finger in her face and wiggled it side to side in order to silence her.

'Do not speak further! Go to the Great Hall and join the feast I have prepared for you to meet prospective suitors,' he commanded. When she refused to move, he snarled, 'Now.'

Catherine reluctantly stepped back from her father. She glared at him as she crossed the study and opened the door, slamming it behind her when she left.

Lord Seymour shook his head and harrumphed.

Once again, Catherine daring to defy him grated on his nerves. He took a few moments to regain his self-control before he plastering on a false smile and wandering out of his study, eager to enjoy the feast.

6

Catherine avoided the Great Hall and wandered the manor to calm her racing thoughts. No matter how she wished to groan about her injuries and sleep for the rest of the day, she had to make an appearance at the feast or that wouldn't be the only argument she'd have with Geoffrey that day. Before she could piece together a plan to find Helena's lair, her stomach rumbled. She patted her empty stomach and sighed. If only to satisfy her hunger, Catherine turned around and walked towards the Great Hall with the intention of getting food and food alone.

Catherine winced as the noise from inside the Hall swept over her like a wave, filling her ears with snippets of gossip and laughter that echoed around the stone room. Metal chimed against metal periodically, which she guessed was the sound of clinking goblets.

She pursed her lips and sighed as she watched her father head straight for the servant handing out drinks. Dealing with her father was hard enough without him having a few goblets of wine in his stomach.

She tilted to head up towards the ceiling, eyes closed, and hoped to God that her father wouldn't make life any harder than he already had.

In the darkness between blinks, Helena's sharp smile flashed and Catherine stiffened.

If the vampire did decide to attend the feast, then at least

Catherine had a chance to figure out where her lair was. Preferably before she could make any of her father's guests her next meal. If Helena wasn't present, well, Catherine would have to find a way to sneak off without getting noticed.

There had to be a way to ensure Birkstead's safety no matter what kind of supernatural entity strolled into the village. Unfortunately, no one had really figured it out yet.

She took a moment to collect herself and walked into the room as if nothing was wrong and she was pleased to be there. It wasn't hard to pretend; she was happy to have the chance to eat.

The smell of hearty meats, wine, and mead flooded her nostrils as she took a few more tentative yet confident steps into the Great Hall. The table in the centre of the room was covered in plates of meat pies, roast lamb, pieces of venison, honeyed carrots, and much more. It looked as delectable as always. The manor chefs refused to disappoint.

She let her skirts fall to the ground, her hem brushing against the red woollen rug taking up most of the stone floor.

A servant dressed in a kirtle as brown as tree bark bowed to Catherine and offered her a goblet of wine, which she took with a small nod in return.

Catherine cradled the goblet in her hand and held it close to her stomach as she stole a glance around the room. She caught the eye of a few nobles who had broken their conversation to watch her stand in the Hall all on her lonesome.

Unwilling to join any of the nobles that had already formed small clusters of conversation, Catherine wandered over to the table proudly displaying the kitchen staff's hard work. She stood close to the table and picked up one of the meat pies that caught her eye. She bit into the pie and watched as the more sociable knights flitted from group to group.

Wine threatened to spill from goblets as easily as the lips of the people around her spilled gossip.

It seemed as if it was going to be just like all the other feasts Lord Geoffrey hosted. At least, until the skin under her silver cross began to prickle from the same chill she felt around Helena.

Panic raced through her mind. She scanned the crowd for the Crusader. Catherine's sociable façade immediately dropped and she moved away from the table, making her way around the Great Hall with the same militant pace she would've adopted on a battlefield. The many layers of her dress slipped between her knees and made it difficult to move with purpose. She had to find the vampire before someone got hurt.

Nobles stared at Catherine with varied mixtures of curiosity and suspicion. Thinking she wasn't paying attention, some whispered about her as she walked past. Most nobles would do their very best to disprove any rumours about them in the most delicate yet petty way possible, but Catherine ignored them entirely. Usually, she delighted in hearing the ridiculous things said about her. She found it hilarious but this time she had no inclination to linger and laugh.

This time was different.

This time, there was at least one vampire among them.

And Catherine seemed to be the only sober knight present.

If said vampire—or even *vampires*—decided that they'd

indulge themself on this free-for-all buffet of blood, Catherine knew for certain fighting would be a death sentence.

Out of the corner of her eye, she spotted a familiar head of copper hair. Her breath left her body as she simultaneously hoped it was and wasn't who she thought it was.

Catherine stopped mid-step and turned to see a smirking Helena surrounded by a gaggle of drunken knights. Her heart leapt into her throat and her stomach fluttered at the sight of Helena in a ruby silk bliaut fit for a royal. A foreign cocktail of disgust at her vampiric nature and attraction to her beauty bubbled within Catherine's chest.

No matter how hard she tried not to be, Catherine was in awe of Helena. The fitted upper sleeve and torso clung to the Crusader in all the right places before the sleeves and the skirt trumpeted out in an ethereal yet impractical way. Her dress swayed as if she were clothed in nothing but shining waterfalls of blood. Helena's fiery hair was bound into two braids by lengths of gold ribbons and laid against her chest either side of her gold and ruby adorned neck. Catherine wondered how Helena came into possession of such finery. She brushed that thought off as she shifted her focus back to ensuring that Helena didn't kill anyone in her family home.

Despite the fact that her skin felt like she'd slept outside on a snowy winter's night, Catherine felt the stunned admiration and infatuation from before crawl its way up her spine and dig its sharp claws into her mind. She put the goblet and pie down to clutch her dagger's hilt. She held onto the weapon so tight that her fingers ached. Her knuckles turned white as she fought to ground herself in reality.

Catherine sauntered over towards the group on the other

side of the room. The knight kept her head held high, her shoulders squared, and her jaw clenched as the vampire's admirers all turned towards Catherine as if she had ruined their chances of winning Helena's affection.

Robert, the youngest of the group, glared at Catherine with shock and outrage as he caught Helena looking her up and down.

'You wear the finery of a noblewoman as well as you do armour, Lady Seymour,' Helena said with a small yet respectful bow of her head. 'I'm quite surprised that you don't have admirers following you wherever you go.'

'Admirers? Her?' Robert exclaimed, pointing at Catherine in disbelief. 'She's lucky that her horse doesn't run away from her.'

Catherine raised an eyebrow at him. Copious amounts of wine made him brave; he was too much of a coward when sober to speak such comments to her face. She rolled her eyes and let his comment stagnate in the silence between them. Catherine turned to respond to Helena's comment, ignoring Robert's for the moment.

'I prefer it this way. In lacking admirers, I can focus on my swordcraft and the needs of the people that rely on my family instead of taking advantage of those who pine for my attention,' Catherine replied, the corner of her top lip quirking upward in irritated revulsion. She turned her ire back towards Robert. 'Besides, I've known Smokey since he was a foal. He wouldn't run away from me even if my face looked as unfortunate as yours.'

Robert's jaw dropped and he swayed slightly as he stepped forward, puffing out his chest like an uncoordinated peacock. He jabbed his finger into Catherine's shoulder as his face reddened. 'What did you say?'

Without changing her expression in the slightest, Catherine balled her hand into a fist and held it against her side so that her skirt hid it from view. She waited for the moment his mouth got him into deeper trouble.

Before Catherine could warn him about keeping his opinions to himself, Helena stepped forward and gently lowered his arm, pulling him back so that she stood in the empty space between the two knights. She stroked his chest and shushed him, mischief twinkling in her crimson eyes and dancing upon her lips.

'Come now, Robert. There's no need to act out. Why don't you and the others go and treat yourselves to more refreshments?' Helena proposed. 'You all worked so hard today, you deserve to reward yourselves.'

Shivers ran down Catherine's spine as she heard the vampire's voice subtly command the desperate knights to leave.

A chorus of disappointed, slurred groans echoed around Helena. Some of the men around her looked genuinely dejected.

Their reaction only served to perk the vampire up even more. She chuckled and turned to face the rest of them, her blood red skirts swishing around her legs. She clasped her hands in front of her stomach and tilted her head with a playful pout.

'I wish to speak with Catherine alone. It's women's business; nothing you'd be interested in. Besides, I'm sure there are other women here simply dying for your attention,' Helena crooned. 'You don't want to disappoint them, do you?'

Sighs and mutters of belligerent acceptance came from the knights as they helped each other over to the refreshments table, where they were instantly met with young noblewomen who gave shy yet hopeful, flirtatious smiles. Within moments, the knights appeared as if they'd forgotten all about the woman they'd been so enamoured with and gorged themselves on food, wine, and the attention of multiple women.

'Like I said, men believe we're nothing more than pawns in their games. They don't expect us to best them.' Helena's pointed smile dazzled Catherine as the vampire attempted to look meek and dainty despite the fangs framing her front teeth. She pressed her lips together and quirked an eyebrow at the other woman in amusement. 'I see you prefer to play their games your way instead of leveraging the rules you've been given. An inspired choice.'

'Why are you here?' Catherine asked.

Despite how uncomfortable the necklace's chill made her, she focused on it to not lose herself in Helena's beauty and charisma. Catherine was unsure whether her vampiric nature was what made Helena so alluring or whether she retained that from her time as a mortal, but it certainly made it harder to remind herself that Helena was one of the only predators that preyed on humans.

Helena's closed smile only widened. 'To socialise, of course. You didn't think I was just going to leave without saying goodbye, did you?'

Catherine frowned. She stepped forward and stared Helena down. Once more, she found herself standing toe to toe with a vampire. Catherine flexed her fingers and grasped hold of her dagger's hilt again, allowing herself to alleviate the ache that came from holding on too tight.

'I know what you are, vampire,' Catherine whispered.

All of the playfulness that brightened Helena's face darkened. It was replaced by an expression as cold as the silver against Catherine's skin. The vampire's crimson eyes glinted with danger while she retained the illusion of being too dainty and feminine to actually cause harm. She pressed her lips together and raised an eyebrow at Catherine.

'Is there somewhere we can speak privately?' Helena asked. 'Without the chance of others hearing?'

Her heart raced at the thought of being alone with the copper-haired beauty. Whether it was because she was going to have the vampire's undivided attention or that she'd have a chance to ensure that Helena was no longer a threat, Catherine couldn't tell. She only had to think for a moment before she knew where she'd take Helena.

'There is. The manor chapel is nearby. Follow me,' Catherine said.

The knight turned on her heel and walked towards the back end of the Hall, glancing over her shoulder to see Helena walking behind her.

Red silk flowed around the vampire's feet, making her steps appear as if she floated across the stone. From what she wore, the way she moved, how she spoke, Helena was ethereal and almost otherworldly.

Everything Helena did made Catherine's heart beat quicker. Her mind was clouded with thoughts of lust; thoughts that she was unsure she could even experience until today.

Though she had found another chance to ensure the safety of those she swore she'd protect from man and monster, Catherine couldn't get the image of Helena's calm, beautiful, dangerous face out of her thoughts. Fresh memories of the vampire's expressions brightened the darkness behind her eyelids every time she blinked.

Catherine touched her mother's cross, the cold grounding her thoughts, but even that sensation couldn't banish the image of Helena's fanged smile from her mind. She gritted her teeth with frustration.

No matter how quiet they attempted to keep their footsteps, both women attracted attention as they left the Hall together. Knights, nobles, and servants alike turned their heads to see Catherine stride out of the hall with the stranger dressed like royalty trailing close behind. Their whispers echoed louder than the thud of the two women's shoes against the stone floors.

The large wooden doors which led out into the hallway slammed shut behind them, silencing the voices that speculated what the future Lady of Birkstead was up to.

7

Catherine held the chapel door open and gestured for Helena to enter first. Even though it wasn't all that dark in the empty hallway, the slight glow emanating from Helena's crimson irises pierced the shadows. Her bruised back prickled as she realised how frightening seeing only two red circles in shining in the darkness would be if she was fearing for her life. That realisation only furthered her desire to protect those who could not defend themselves. And yet, she couldn't help but to find it amusing that Helena didn't want to walk into a room completely alone with Catherine despite being an apex predator.

'Scared of a holy room, are we?' Catherine teased, a small smirk touching her lips.

Helena's frown deepened as she stared into the chapel.

'Sacred grounds do nothing to vampires,' she replied. 'I'm wary of this being a trap.'

'Even if it was a trap, you'd easily be able to outrun or overpower whatever I had waiting in there. All the knights we both bested are at the feast, indulging themselves in drink and food. If I tried anything, you could dispatch me in seconds and get a meal out of it too,' Catherine reasoned. 'You have nothing to lose.'

Despite the fact Catherine presented sound logic, Helena still eyed her with uncertainty. She stared at the knight and walked into the room, glancing at the corners of the chapel briefly to see if Catherine indeed was telling the truth. She didn't have to wait long before the heavy wooden door was closed. Her red silk skirts twisted around her legs as she turned to take in the room and the woman she'd bested.

Helena glanced along the back wall, noticing the stone cross that decorated the wall behind the altar. The vampire dropped her hands by her side and watched Catherine's hands closely, especially the hand that clutched her dagger.

Catherine widened her stance as she noticed how Helena embodied the skittish and cautious nature of a fruit bat instead of a monster capable of slaughtering an entire town. No matter the fact that she had willingly put herself in danger, the lone human in the room found it amusing that the two of them were sizing each other up as if it they could have an equal fight.

'You got what you asked for. No one else is here. There is no chance that your admirers will find out that the woman they fawned over is not only the warrior who unhorsed them, but is also a vampire.'

Before she could ask Helena what she wanted to say now that they had the privacy she requested, the vampire sped across the room faster than Catherine could blink.

Without any warning, Helena slammed the knight's back against the altar, wrapping her hand around Catherine's neck. The edge of her hand turned red as her skin made contact with the necklace that caressed Catherine's collarbone.

Pain lanced through Catherine's back and aggravated the bruises tingeing her skin dark purple. Her lungs burned and, despite the futility of doing so, she gasped for breath as Helena's grasp slowly tightened around her windpipe. Tears welled in her eyes. Her eyeballs threatened to pop out of her skull. She gritted her teeth and strained her sides attempting to wriggle out of Helena's vice grip. She wrestled with the vampire's skirts to free her dagger from its sheath.

Danger glinted in the darkness of Helena's pupils. Her beautiful face was contorted with quiet fury. The bridge of her nose crinkled and her lips peeled back to reveal her incredibly sharp fangs. She squeezed Catherine's neck tighter and leant closer to the veins that pulsed underneath her hand, grimacing as Catherine's chain charred her skin. No matter how much the silver burned, Helena was not going to let go.

'I've never had a knight's blood before,' Helena purred. The vampire ran her free hand down the side of Catherine's face and darkly chuckled. 'I suppose there's a first time for everything, isn't there?'

Catherine's heart raced and fear finally ran rampant through her mind. And yet, she couldn't ignore the small part of her that wanted to see if Helena's fangs got in the way when she kissed someone.

She clamped her eyes shut and shook that thought from the forefront of her mind, focusing on prying Helena's hand from her throat enough to take a breath before she passed out. But when Helena's tongue ran up a vein in her neck and positioned her fangs, ready to pierce her flesh, she forgot she needed to breathe at all.

Catherine gasped as Helena's razor-sharp fangs glided across her skin. Her body stirred with desire, forcing her fear to be absorbed by a completely new, dominating emotion she didn't recognise.

Helena bit down. She dragged her tongue across the blood that welled around her fangs, savouring the bittersweet flavour touching her tastebuds.

Catherine's eyes widened as the intense rush of pleasure and pain overwhelmed her thoughts and forced her body to shudder.

The utterly delicious moan that left Catherine's lips caught Helena by surprise almost as much as it did the knight herself.

Helena froze, fangs still embedded in her neck. She did not expect such a sound to come from Catherine.

The vampire's grip relaxed around Catherine's throat and she pulled her lips away. Helena's smirk grew wider as she pressed a finger against the patch of skin just underneath the knight's jaw. The burn on the side of her hand began to heal as the knight's blood coursed through her system.

Catherine coughed as she struggled to breathe past the sensation of swallowing imaginary needles.

Though she had the chance to take control of the situation, Catherine didn't take advantage of it. She was just too stunned by what had taken place.

She remained underneath Helena, her eyes wide and her heart pounding. Butterflies fluttered around in her stomach. Her lower belly tensed and warmed without warning.

'Odd, but delicious.' Helena licked Catherine's blood from her lips, arching an eyebrow at her. 'Surely this isn't the first time you've experienced some form of carnal pleasure?'

Catherine didn't answer.

She finally unsheathed her dagger, slashing the

vampire's wrist whilst she was distracted by the lust that stirred within Catherine's body.

The blade sliced through the red silk and Helena's flesh. The vampire's skin sizzled and smoked.

The vampire screamed as the veins around the wound turned black as coal. Though the damage wasn't anywhere near enough to kill her, it sure hurt like it could.

Helena's screech echoed around the stone room with the intensity of a thousand bats fleeing the light of the rising sun. Her sleeve darkened with blood. Her beautiful face was contorted in animalistic pain as she fell over the top of a pew and onto the floor.

The stench of burning flesh lingered around the altar.

Catherine gasped and coughed, breathing in too much air for her aching lungs to handle. She placed one hand on the altar underneath her to steady herself as her knees collapsed out from underneath her.

Anticipating the vampire's quick recovery and retaliation, Catherine held her dagger out in front of herself while she regained her breath. She clamped her free hand against the bite on her neck to stanch the bleeding.

'Stay back! I will not let you cloud my mind, foul blood-sucker,' Catherine declared, barely able to speak between gasps. 'Your mind tricks won't work on me.'

Clutching her wounded wrist, Helena forced herself to her feet. The vampire bared her fangs with a feral hiss. She glared at Catherine from underneath her browbone; her red eyes glowing ominously in the shadows that shrouded her face. Her smirk returned to her face moments later. Helena kept her hand wrapped around her forearm as she circled Catherine, who staggered to her feet in front of the altar.

The vampire's skin started to knit back together. The healing process stung so much that tears welled in the corners of her eyes. Pus and blood wept from the gash in her arm and seeped into her silk sleeves, corrupting its flawless crimson sheen.

'Unlike your compatriots in the Great Hall, I've only made myself appear more human around you. Whatever you accuse me of making you feel is all you,' Helena replied. The remnants of Catherine's blood continued to please her palate in ways that she couldn't put into words. 'You may not find this comforting, but your blood is strange yet delicious. It doesn't taste like any other human I've drank from before.'

Catherine gritted her teeth and stumbled forwards, thrusting her dagger in the vampire's direction. 'You're right, I don't find that comforting at all.'

Helena's laugh rang through the chapel like a bell, loud and melodic.

The sound of her voice sent Catherine's thoughts reeling.

The vampire took a step towards the knight, careful to avoid being in swiping distance of the dagger. She tilted her chin down to appear both innocent and playful as she chuckled at Catherine's frustration.

'Contrary to how threatening it sounds, having delicious blood gives me a good incentive to keep you alive. If you are drained dry, I'd have to travel far and wide to find another mortal as tasty and pretty as you. That's too much trouble.' Helena pouted. 'And why would I want to cause more trouble than I need

61

to?'

'Because that's what vampires do,' Catherine replied, glaring at Helena.

Helena turned her back to Catherine and walked down the aisle towards the door. She glanced over her shoulder at the knight. 'If all vampires caused more trouble than needed, there'd be a world-wide epidemic of vampire-related deaths, wouldn't there?'

Before Catherine could form a reply, the vampire vanished.

The wooden door creaked closed.

Catherine lowered her dagger as she stared at the empty space Helena stood moments before. All of the thoughts that she pushed off in order to focus on survival flooded her mind.

She wasn't surprised by the fact that her thoughts decided to overwhelm her, but she was surprised by the lustful ones that revolved around Helena.

Helena was a vampire, but Catherine was unsure if she would want to defend herself if Helena stood over her again with that cocky smirk of hers. Catherine didn't even know if she could stop herself from seeing if Helena's lips were as soft as they looked. Did undeath affect how soft someone's skin was?

She shook her head, hoping that the movement would dissipate the hot blush and lust-fuelled thoughts disrupting her clarity. In all her years, she'd never felt so flustered and tongue-tied over anyone before. Even when she found someone attractive, she still had some control over her thoughts.

It was different with Helena.

A Knight's Blood

Catherine had no idea why.

Despite the fact that she was bleeding and bruised, Catherine knew that she had to return to the gathering in the Great Hall after seeing the healer. People were talking when she left with Helena and Catherine had to come back in order to silence the rumours about herself. That and she and Walter were supposed to patrol Birkstead's outskirts that night.

With Helena out and able to wander around unhindered once the sun went down, Catherine felt it was more important than ever to be at her best to protect the people. Even if all she wanted to do was sleep until her flesh was no longer splotched purple and blue.

8

The feeble flame that flickered atop Walter's torch did little to keep the night's chill at bay. Their only source of heat and light glimmered with tendrils of orange and yellow. Smoke twirled up into the darkness of the night above.

Catherine's skin prickled underneath the layers of her armor as the cold enclosed her in its embrace. While the sensation was uncomfortable, she enjoyed seeing fog float from their mouths and dissipate into the air.

When she turned her head to the left, she could see warm glows emanating from Birkstead's windows. Catherine sat back in her saddle and let out a small sigh as she watched some houses go dark. She raised her head to the heavens and watched the stars twinkle against the night's dark shroud.

The moon was bright and round, mimicking the widened pupils of a child caught in wonderous thought. The moon and her sparkling court watched over Catherine as she continued honouring her vow with glee.

While she didn't grow up in the village itself, her family were responsible for their protection. Her ancestors presided over Birkstead for the last century after the previous noble house was removed from power after the civil war. Once Birkstead was rebuilt, the village flourished. The only scar that remained from that time was the broken church half an hour's ride away from the village square. Her great-grandfather didn't see the need to repair it and built a smaller chapel just off the village square in order to strengthen the community's bond between each other and God. Thankfully, it did just that and wasn't considered a waste of resources as his advisors had claimed. The old church, however, was left to ruin on the outskirts of the village.

Birkstead sat in the shadows of the Seymour manor, allowing the knights nearby to reach the village with great haste should anyone, or anything, decide to attack. The village itself was comprised of the chapel, a courtyard big enough to host markets when merchants travelled through, small stores selling bread and other goods sat on the edge of said courtyard, and homes clustered together a short walk from it all. Most of the buildings were constructed from rough stone and decorated with wooden beams that had been painted by the children that resided inside with their parents.

Walter's horse, a dappled-grey mare named Miriam, shook her mane and huffed as a fly buzzed around her ear.

'Whoa there,' he said, bringing Miriam to a stop. He let go of the reins and waved his hand around her ears to shoo the bug away. He patted her neck and picked up the reins again. 'There you go, that's better.'

The two horses walked side by side as their riders scanned the areas between the sparse stone buildings that made up the village. They clopped through the village square, ears turning when they heard quiet conversations and movements coming from inside the buildings nearby. Nothing Smokey or Miriam heard spooked them, so they continued forward at a lazy pace.

'It's quiet tonight,' Catherine remarked, glancing at Walter.

He sniffled, his large bushy moustache trembling upon

65

his lip. 'That it is. Perhaps the beasts have decided to stay with their offspring instead of terrorising livestock?'

She couldn't help but to smile at her old mentor. The good-hearted knight found light in even the darkest circumstance.

'I hope so. I heard whispers that the ewes are due to give birth in the next few days. The people deserve some good news to alleviate their fear.'

Walter's smile faded slightly as he cleared his throat. 'Aye, they do. Especially since there was a vampire scare two towns over, they're all on edge.'

Catherine stiffened at the mention of a vampire attack. Was Helena responsible?

'That's uncomfortably close. What measures do we have to protect the people when vampires decide to attack?' Catherine asked, trying her hardest not to immediately panic him with the news of a vampire's presence.

The old knight sighed. He pursed his lips as he moved the torch back and forth, dispersing the light around them.

'There's not much we can do. We know vampires are weak to silver, hawthorn, and yew. Decapitating and burning the body is the best way to destroy them. Unless we have a way to trap the vampire and then dispatch them, there is no reliable way to keep vampires from entering the village. Patrols like the one we have tonight are the only way we can spook the more cowardly bloodsuckers away,' Walter replied. 'The more hardened mercenaries go for the Church's bounty to help thin out the herd, but that's about it.'

She had a feeling her mother could've told her more, but

she was unsure if any of her findings survived her death.

Catherine patted Smokey's neck and sighed as they continued to patrol Birkstead's outer edges for anything that would prey on the vulnerable villagers that resided there. So far, everything was quiet and calm.

Catherine knew that serenity wouldn't last.

Her thoughts of Helena hadn't gone away after their tense encounter in the manor's chapel. Almost as if her thoughts had summoned the vampire, her cross grew cold once more.

'The Church were the ones to put bounties in place; asking for the ashes and fangs of any vampires in exchange for gold. I can't bear to think of how many people died in the pursuit of that reward,' Catherine replied.

Walter shook his head, clicking his tongue quickly. It was his favourite way of discreetly cautioning her. 'I know you mean well, but please be careful what you say about the Church in front of others. Some don't take kindly to its integrity being questioned.'

'I know. I just don't believe that their intentions are solely reserved for honouring God,' Catherine replied.

'Though that is the truth, I still implore you to beware who you speak to in regards to the Church. Good people have been hurt for simply questioning how things are,' Walter added.

She opened her mouth to say something, but lost the thought. She pressed her lips together and adjusted her grip on her reins to keep herself quiet. Not wishing to dwell on the concern that was plastered all over her mentor's face, she turned her attention back to surveying the village since her necklace continued to chill her chest.

The pathways to the city centre were almost as dark as the night sky itself. Without sunlight and the hustle and bustle of people at market, an air of eeriness blanketed the empty space. If it weren't for the fact that Catherine knew a vampire was somewhere nearby, the silence would've been welcome. Instead, Catherine couldn't shake the suspicion that something was in the darkness, waiting for the right time to strike.

Shivers ran up and down her arms as they let their horses leisurely plod along the road.

Walter let out a loud yawn and shook his head to dispel sleep's grasp for as long as he could.

Even though Catherine's intuition stirred the butterflies in her stomach and wanted her to remain alert, her exhaustion and pain started to take over.

Unfortunately for the two knights, dawn was still a long time coming.

'I hope the kitchens have some hot stew for us when we get back. I could do with warm food to get the chill out of these bones,' Walter said, a bright smile returning to his kind face.

She nodded. 'Me too. Either that, or a lit fireplace. I'm sore and all I wish to do is sleep.'

Before Walter even got to agree with her, loud violent hissing overpowered his torch's crackling. He brought his steed to a halt and swung his torch around, looking for the source of the sound.

Catherine stopped Smokey beside Miriam and placed her hand on her sword's hilt. She held herself as still as possible so she could focus on pinpointing what made that sound. A frown touched her brow.

Smokey dug his hoof into the dirt, kicking a rock in the process.

She couldn't make out most of what was being said. The only words she caught came from a heavily-accented masculine voice calling someone else "a venomous whore", and that someone else calling the other a "coward" with a sultry, feminine growl.

It was clear that they—whatever they were—weren't friendly towards each other. That was concerning in itself. But what Catherine found more concerning was the fact that the feminine growl sounded familiar.

Catherine's heart pounded harder.

Walter swung his torch towards the chapel, casting some light to chase away the darkness that enshrouded the holy building.

Miriam shied away from the chapel, snorting.

Shadows danced in the light, disappearing as quickly as they appeared.

The sound of clashing blades rang out, filling the air with the chaotic symphony of battle.

The old knight turned towards Catherine.

Vampires.

The crack of breaking stone echoed through the village, followed by the familiar screech of metal against metal. Groans and cursing were only just heard over the chapel's back wall.

The clashing of swords began again before any normal human could've recovered and reacted.

The knights steered their horses towards the chapel to survey the damage and potentially catch the culprits that disturbed the peace. Most of the stone wall had been demolished. It was a miracle the roof didn't collapse with it. Pebbles slid across the chapel floor and the crack of splitting wood echoed against the remaining stone walls.

Catherine's heart beat hard and fast against her ribcage. Her hand trembled ever so slightly as she moved it towards the dagger strapped to her belt instead of her trusty sword.

Smokey whinnied and shied away from the chapel's newly collapsed wall, flattening his ears against his head and snorting in rapid succession.

Not giving into fear, Walter spurred Miriam on, getting as close to the damage as his horse would allow.

'Be careful,' she whispered.

Walter dismounted and held his torch out in front of him, angling the flames so that it illuminated as much of the chapel as possible. The splintering of wood and the shattering of glass continued to echo around him. A pair of shadows that moved faster than he could blink. No matter how hard he tried to define their features, they were much too quick for him to be able to see anything other than their outlines and the sudden gleam of their weapons.

Not wanting to leave her mentor by himself, Catherine edged her horse closer to the gaping hole in the chapel wall. She, too, had trouble seeing anything definitive. She caught a glimpse of shining red and blond hair before they vanished from the torch's glow.

Catherine got off her horse and unsheathed her dagger with her left hand. Her steps echoed around the remaining chapel walls as she crept to Walter's side. She kicked a dented chalice across the floor and cringed as it pinged against a nearby wall.

Walter whipped his head around and placed his finger to his lips, urging her to remain silent. While the pair of them could've handled one vampire, two was almost certainly a death sentence.

The pair of shadows stopped in the darkness at the back of the chapel. Two sets of glowing red eyes appeared.

Catherine and Walter looked at each other. Without the element of surprise, two humans were helpless against two vampires, no matter how great their training was or how many silver weapons they wielded. Both knights unsheathed their swords and held them steady, careful not to let fear overwhelm their thoughts.

Catherine adjusted her grip to comfortably wield her sword in her right and her dagger in her left.

Walter held his torch tighter and drew in a deep breath.

Before they could take a step forward, the glowing eyes disappeared and the shadows lunged. They looked around the room to try and gauge where the two vampires were going to attack from.

Catherine swallowed what little saliva she had in her mouth. The cold continued to prickle her flesh underneath her armour. Her foggy breath obscured part of her vision, making it hard to pinpoint where the vampires were. She crossed one foot over the other, slowly moving towards the back of the chapel, weapons raised. Her hearing was hindered by her pulse thundering in her ears.

One moment, they were alone in their little bubble of light; the next, Walter cried out as he was knocked to the ground. His torch was ripped from his hand and the flame was snuffed by a stomp from a forceful black boot.

Catherine caught a glimpse of a pale-faced blond man with teeth sharper than daggers. His blood-red eyes were framed by streaks of black war paint.

She moved towards Walter to help him to his feet, but was swept off hers and thrown out onto the dirt outside the chapel. The impact stole the air from her body. Her bruises stung. Pain shot up her shoulders and down her spine.

It was moments like these in which she despised wearing armour.

One of the vampires perched themselves on her chest and held a sharp blade against her throat.

Catherine tried not to swallow her spittle as the vampire hissed down at her. Soft locks of hair brushed against the knight's cheek as the vampire leant down towards her neck, laughing with their teeth bared. The sweetest laugh she'd heard only once before.

'Fancy seeing you here,' a familiar voice crooned.

She set her weight upon the knight's tabard to keep her pinned to the ground.

'Get off me, Helena,' Catherine spat.

She shook her head at the human underneath her. 'Then

stay out of my way,' she hissed in reply. 'You both should've run.'

The knight twisted and slashed Helena's thigh with her dagger.

The vampire hissed and leapt off her.

Catherine heaved in a deep breath as the sound of bubbling flesh filled her ears.

Helena fled into the chapel's darkest corner, her glowing eyes glaring straight at Catherine.

Catherine breathed as deeply as she could and she leant on her sword to get back on her feet. She turned towards a yelp that came from behind her and stopped. Her eyes widened in shock.

The other vampire held Walter up in the air by the back of his neck, his feet dangling above the ground.

Catherine's throat scratched as terror and panic gripped her body and forced her to do the one thing she hated: freeze. No matter how she willed herself to move, she couldn't.

Walter's arms flailed as he attempted to stab the vampire. The longer he was suspended by his neck, the more fatigued his swings got. His scream was cut short by the vampire's bite.

The vampire clamped their teeth upon his throat and tore it from his body. They spat the chunk of flesh out and laughed as Walter's body went limp. They bit their tongue and spat into the knight's open mouth.

Sickened by what she'd seen, Catherine inched towards where Walter was being suspended with her dagger and sword pointed at the grinning monster still holding him.

The shadow that held Walter up vanished into the darkness as she got closer, dropping the old knight like an angry child drops a ragdoll.

In that moment, Catherine didn't care that the vampires had gotten away. All she cared about was Walter.

She ran to his side.

He lay motionless on the ground.

She dropped to her knees beside him, wincing as she pulled him up onto her lap. Keeping her breathing steady became difficult as she searched for any signs of life.

There was no movement from his nostrils or his mouth or his throat.

Blood slickened his neck and face. It dripped onto Catherine before it trickled down to the ground underneath her.

'Walter?' Her voice caught in her throat. 'Walter, please stay with me.'

Tears welled as she stared into his lifeless eyes.

What little blood was left in him trickled down onto her armour and slickened the stone underneath them.

Catherine clutched him close and let the tears fall down her cheeks. Seeing his almost paper-thin skin marred by puncture wounds and his missing throat hurt more than she cared to verbalise. One by one, her tears fell from her face to his tabard. Sobs wracked her body. Catherine felt as if her world had crumbled like the chapel's wall.

A Knight's Blood

She wanted to stay there and let her tears wash away his blood from his face.

No matter how much she wanted to stay there on her knees and mourn the loss of her mentor, she knew it wouldn't be safe to do so. The longer she stayed, the larger the chance that Helena and the other vampire would return to kill her too.

There was also the risk that Walter could reawaken as a vampire himself. One bite was not enough to create a new vampire. The person bitten would have to have swallowed a vampire's blood in return. The vampire who killed Walter spat in his mouth and Catherine had no way of knowing if there was blood in it or not.

Catherine knew what she was expected to do. She didn't know if she could even bring herself to do it.

'I'm sorry,' she mumbled.

She placed his head back down upon the ground. Tears continued to stream down her face as she picked up her sword. Catherine moved back to allow some room for the blade to hit what was left of Walter's neck to sever it without much struggle. She raised her sword high above her head.

Before she brought down the sword, she glanced down at Walter. She folded her lips between her teeth as she bit back the guilt that wracked her brain.

Mutilating the body of the man that taught her so much about the world and herself felt like the ultimate betrayal. If only she'd mentioned she knew there was a vampire among them, perhaps Walter would be alive. She closed her eyes and turned her head to the side, reminding herself that he could come back as the monster that killed him.

Memories of Walter flooded the dark void behind her

eyelids. She recalled the first time he handed her a wooden sword, him teaching her how to ride a horse, how to hold herself with pride while wearing armour heavier than she was. Whenever Catherine needed help and her father refused to even acknowledge her problems, Walter was always there to assist her with a warm smile and a hug.

Decapitating the man who had been her strongest parental figure growing up hurt more than falling from Smokey ever could.

The sobs she attempted to keep at bay returned and she let her arms flop down by her sides. Her chest ached from lack of breath.

She couldn't do it.

'I'm so sorry,' she repeated, her words shaky.

Catherine hauled Walter's body up off the ground and placed him gingerly over Smokey's saddle. Her breaths hitched and her chest shuddered. After standing beside her horse for a few moments, she patted him on the neck and picked up his reins, ready to let her tears fall once she had walked Smokey down the road.

Caked up to her knees in blood and cold night air nipping at her tear-stained cheeks, Catherine began the trek back to the manor, praying that she would get back before dawn.

9

Her father's office smelt of wood and leather with the smallest hint of mead. Tapestries of coloured wool hung from either side of the heavy wooden desk, each depicting fearsome beasts and the knights that would slay them. The stone floors were adorned with woollen rugs dyed a green deeper than pine needles. Pages upon pages of paper were scattered over his desk.

She turned and stared at the fireplace behind her, watching the flames flicker against its confinement to keep herself together. Catherine was still clad in her armour, her shins painted with Walter's dried blood.

No matter how she tried, she could not banish the image of the dark figure with copper hair from her mind. She clenched her teeth and fought back the tears that irritated her bloodshot eyes. Even focusing on that couldn't keep her attention for long; her thoughts always returned to Helena.

Aldric placed his hand on her shoulder. He tried his best not to smile sadly when she turned to look at him, but failed. His kind topaz eyes regarded her with worry. An old scar ran across his nose, the tissue shiny and mottled.

'I know it's been a hard night, Cat, but please don't let your fatigue and grief cloud your judgement. You know how your father is,' he said.

'Thank you for the reminder,' she replied, gritting her teeth at the thought of seeing her father again.

'Sir Alwyn was a wonderful man. He will be deeply missed,' Aldric said with a sigh. 'What happened?'

'Vampires. Their scuffle destroyed the Birkstead chapel. One of them killed Walter,' Catherine replied and forced herself to stand up straight.

His face fell and his eyes widened. Aldric glanced around the room and leant closer to Catherine, keeping his voice low. 'Vampires? Truly?'

She looked into his eyes, noticing his reluctance to look at hers. She nodded. 'Truly.'

'Did you get a good look at them?' Aldric asked.

She went to ask him what he meant by that but stopped herself when she heard her father stomping towards the room.

The door swung open and Lord Seymour stormed into his study.

'Close the door,' he commanded.

She walked over to the door and closed it, sliding the latch in place. Catherine stood there a second too long as she let out a deep breath and approached the desk with her hands clasped in front of her, appearing much like she would in court.

Whatever warmth there had been between father and daughter had long since been extinguished, likely never to return.

'You wished to speak to me?' Catherine asked.

Geoffrey started to pick up the papers that were scattered over his desk and put them all into a pile to his right. He didn't even look up at her.

A Knight's Blood

'What happened?' he snapped. 'My best knight is dead and the village chapel is destroyed!'

She fought back tears with a deep breath. Catherine would rather hold a sword by its blade with her bare hand than have her father see her cry.

Aldric saw the pain on her face and fought the urge to take her into his arms and give her the hug her father would never give her. He clenched his jaw as he waited for Catherine to explain.

'There was a disturbance. Two vampires were locked in combat with each other. Sir Alwyn and I went to investigate the damage when one of them fled and I attempted to pursue while he looked for the other. He was overpowered and drained of blood. I came back to assist him, but it was too late.'

Geoffrey's brow and nose scrunched in frustration. He clasped his hands together and propped his elbows up on his desk. An exasperated sigh fell from his lips as he shook his head. He kept his gaze trained on the letters in his hands instead of looking up at the knights standing on the other side of his desk.

'I don't care for what you found. I care about the fact that it's going to cost a fortune to rebuild the chapel. Taxes will have to be raised again to afford the repairs.'

She narrowed her eyes at her father and pursed her lips. 'We have more than enough in our treasury for the repairs. What I'm more concerned about is that the people are in danger and you don't seem to care.'

'That's what we have knights for, Catherine. It's your duty to protect the people from harm,' Geoffrey scolded. 'From what I remember, you were the one who pleaded to be one and I relented, believing you'd fall into line and do what's expected of

79

you when you realised your mistake.'

Catherine puffed out her chest ever so slightly as she tilted her head and smiled a courtly smile; one that made her appear sweet but didn't reach her eyes. Anger swept through her body. She delighted in the fantasy of reaching across the desk and grabbing her father by his neck.

'You can't be serious,' Catherine said with a shake of her head. 'Raising taxes causes more problems than it solves.'

The other knight looked at the young lady standing up to her father. Aldric raised an eyebrow at how blunt Catherine was.

'Sir Carey, I do not wish to hear you agreeing with her on this,' Geoffrey said, glaring at the older knight. 'You know how expensive it is to pay workers and get the resources needed to rebuild even the smallest building. Don't feed into her idealistic delusions.'

The older knight opened his mouth to speak but thought better of it when Geoffrey glared at him.

'I mean it. Don't encourage her or I will stop funding your daughter's education,' Geoffrey threatened.

Aldric pressed his lips together and nodded in reluctant agreement.

While he admired that Catherine was almost fearless in speaking her mind, Aldric had a family to look after. He couldn't afford to upset the man who paid for his daughter's education. Shame twisted in his stomach as he glanced down at the floor.

Geoffrey shifted his ire from Aldric back to Catherine. He looked her up and down, a distasteful frown dragging his lips downward. Geoffrey removed his elbows from the desk and stood up, attempting to loom over his daughter.

'What we do with the people's taxes is none of your concern, Catherine.'

The fire crackled and popped in the silence that followed. Fat droplets hit the window panes, trickling down as another raindrop took its place. The crops would welcome more rain, but all Catherine could think about was how it would wash away Walter's blood.

She was done restraining herself for her father's sake.

'Well, my lord, forgive me for speaking in areas in which I am meant to be ignorant,' Catherine said with a venomous sneer. 'I may be a knight, but I am of your blood. Your people are my people. I swore to protect them and protect them I shall, even if I have to from you.'

One of Catherine's dark braids fell against her cheek as she tilted her head slightly, waiting for her father's response.

Him refusing to speak was usually a sign of trouble for those who wished to stay in his good graces.

Catherine was not one of those people.

Pride swelled in her chest. Her sneer morphed into a malicious smirk as she met his glare with her own, challenging him to prove her wrong.

Geoffrey gritted his teeth and sighed, lowering his gaze in defeat.

'You have a point,' he conceded. 'Birkstead would not be able to function without its people.'

'You need the people as much as they need a strong

leader. My lord, you owe it to them to ensure that they're protected and their place of worship is restored without impacting
their way of life even further.'

'Catherine, I want you to find what caused this damage
and put them down. If it was indeed vampires, collect the fangs
and the ashes of the two burned corpses and we'll claim the
Pope's bounty on behalf of the people. I'll give you a week to
find what did this and deal with it.'

Catherine nodded in agreement, excited to finally have a
chance to prove herself even if the task was daunting. 'Yes, my
lord.'

Geoffrey turned to look at Aldric.

'And you,' he said, pointing at the knight. 'I know you
want to help Catherine. I appreciate it. However, she needs to
do this on her own. Offer her advice but that's all. She needs to
learn how to handle difficult tasks on her own.'

Aldric remained silent as he nodded in reply.

A smirk as prideful as his daughter's graced his face.
'And I'll start arranging a marriage for Catherine in the mean-
time. If you believe that you have the knowledge to govern the
village better than I can, then it's time for you to ensure that our
lineage continues on.'

Her smile fell and she instinctively reached out for the
cross around her neck, running her thumb across the engraved
metal. She knew it was a matter of time before he pushed his
plans for her future onto her with more force, but she didn't think
that he'd do so this soon.

'Father-'

Geoffrey held his hand up and shook his head,

dismissing her before she could continue speaking.

'You've just seen your twenty-second winter. I gave you time to pursue your training with Sir Alwyn but it's time for you to do your duty as a noblewoman. While our name won't go down to the next generation, Birkstead goes to someone regardless and I'd rather keep it in the family,' Geoffrey announced.

No matter how hard she tried, she could not convince him that she was meant for more than just being someone's wife. The knight continued to rub the cross that hung from her neck, wondering if her mother would've had better luck convincing him otherwise.

'Yes, my lord,' she reluctantly replied. 'On the stipulation that should I obtain the two sets of vampiric remains, I get to choose who I marry.'

'Very well. Get started on your little investigation. If there's no results by the end of the week, I'll find someone who can get them. You're free to go,' Geoffrey waved his hand to shoo her out of his office before he gestured for Aldric to approach his desk.

The other knight gave Catherine a small smile and a pat on the back before he stepped forward.

Catherine gave her father a small curtsey and left the office, slamming the door behind her.

The world around her span. Her heart beat as if she were in the heat of battle. The weight of Walter's death and her father's expectations proved too much to handle all at once.

She drew in a breath through her nose and stared at the door as if she could rip it off its hinges with her eyes.

Though there weren't many fellow nobles or knights

milling around in the main foyer, Catherine still plucked up the energy to create a façade that hid her emotions and smiled as she hurried down the winding hallways towards the kitchens.

A week was not a lot of time. She took a few moments to compose herself before she even thought about what she should do next. She needed to at least be able to protect herself properly if she came across any vampires.

Catherine quickly closed the door to the kitchen, trying her very best not to think of copper hair, blood, or crimson eyes that pierced the dark.

10

Despite sleeping for hours, Catherine felt as if she had been awake for days on end. Her grief-addled thoughts made her more sluggish than her sore muscles ever could. Catherine swept her hands up her face and down through her messy braids with a sigh. Her emotions crashed against one another, violent and dangerous like the ocean in a ferocious storm. Some of the bruises from the tournament had darkened to purple. Her hands trembled even as the fire roared in its hearth.

Catherine closed her eyes and grasped her mother's cross. There, in what should've been pure darkness behind her eyelids, was the image that haunted her sleep: a pair of red glowing eyes that followed her no matter where she turned and copper hair breaking up the darkness as if the strands were made of fire. No matter how she tried, fear and arousal battled for dominance whenever she thought of the Crusader.

Heart pounding, she opened her eyes and let her hand fall away from the pendant. Catherine mentally scolded herself for letting Helena get into her head like that. Never before had she been so attracted to someone, let alone someone who craved human blood.

Catherine put on a pair of pants and a tunic as if she were going out to train in the courtyard. With both her sword and dagger strapped to her belt, she made her way out of her bedroom and wandered towards the stables outside, stopping at the armoury to pick up her shield. Her feet dragged against the stone floors. Her legs were heavy with exhaustion.

Even though she wanted to start her quest as soon as she could, Catherine kept up appearances; nodding to the nobles that visited the manor as she walked by. She made it seem as if mourning the loss of her mentor was the only emotion distracting her.

The nobles milling around the Seymour manor, dressed in their resplendent furs and jewels, smiled and acknowledged her in return. These visitors appeared to have not a care in the world, smiling and laughing as they conversed about silly mistakes their servants made and gossiped about their peers. For the wealthy and carefree, life continued on as normal.

The pain of slowly losing everything she held dear tore her apart. It hurt more than she could explain to hide her grief. She kept her chin up to appear as if her happiness and pride had not been smashed to pieces, hiding her bloodshot eyes with the shadows covering her face.

Plans of where to go and what to investigate first clouded Catherine's mind to a point where she began to lose sense of what was around her. Her tired, puffy eyes could barely focus on anything and anyone. The fuzziness from when she woke up hadn't fully dissipated. Features on the different faces she forced herself to smile at were undisguisable from one another.

She was a snail in a cyclone, moving slowly as the world around her blurred and swirled without end.

As soon as she stepped outside, the sun streamed into her eyes and banished the fog that gripped her journey to the stables. She raised her hand to her face, resting the side of her fingers against her brow to let her eyes adjust to the light. Though that first breath of air outside the stuffy manor was usually enough to calm her, Catherine still felt the manor's suffocating grasp upon her mind. Grief and sorrow, as all-encompassing and intense as they were on their own, weren't all that affected her thoughts. The risk of failing of her father's task and having to marry who he chose for her threatened to destroy any sense of normalcy she had left.

Thankfully, Catherine still had some constants she could rely on to keep herself grounded when her world was beginning to fall apart. Smokey, her horse, was one of them.

Smokey waited in the stable for her arrival. She patted his neck and tacked him up to leave. Once he was ready, she led him out of the stable and onto the manor grounds. She pulled herself into the saddle and spurred him on through the land her family had staked as their home.

Relief washed over her as the manor disappeared behind her and she ended up on the road just outside Birkstead. Even though the manor was out of sight, she still felt as if its claws were embedded into her shoulders. Catherine had to begin looking for the vampires soon or there'd be no chance in Hell she'd be able to obtain the fangs and ashes she needed before the week was out. That much was obvious. However, she wanted to get as far away from the manor as possible.

The sun warmed the sides of her face as she wondered where she could begin her search. Catherine was sure that unless Helena decided to wear her Crusader armour out and about, both vampires wouldn't want to be out during the day unless they wanted their skin to blister and burn until it cracked and flaked off in chunks.

She hated the idea of putting herself in a monster's shoes, but she had to if she wished to find them. If she were a vampire that wanted shelter from the sun and also wanted to remain close to a supply of blood, where would she go? It didn't take her long to come to a conclusion.

The old ruined church outside Birkstead.

11

The path leading to the collapsing church was washed away by years of rain and overgrown with weeds.

She glanced over her shoulder to see how far the village appeared from the church's gates. The tallest buildings looked no bigger than her thumbnail. The odd sheep she could pick out looked like clouds that decided to come down from the sky and play upon the land. Their bleats were carried towards her by the wind, fading to a faint echo by the time they reached her ears.

Cool spring air brushed her cheeks and pulled wisps of dark hair out of the knight's braids.

Her smile fell from her face as she turned back to examine the church ruins. What was once a beautiful place of congregational prayer had been left to rot, forgotten in favour of something newer and closer to home.

The tower that once held the bells had collapsed, leaving stones scattered amongst the grass. Patches of said grass had turned yellow from lack of sunlight. Whatever stained glass had been in the windows were either shattered from the civil unrest near the end of the last century or salvaged for new for the chapel her great-grandfather built in Birkstead. Half of the roof had caved in, whether it was damage done due to the unrest or time and the weather, Catherine didn't know. The stones that supported the structure itself were covered in moss. Vines half-heartedly crawled up the corners of the building, not reaching any farther than her horse's knees. Broken headstones stood among the field of weeds, marking what was left of the graveyard.

The closer she got to the building, the more uneasy she felt.

Smokey flattened his ears against his head and slowed down to a stop outside the broken stone fence.

'I know,' she said, soothing Smokey with a rub on his neck. 'Something feels wrong.'

Catherine dismounted and tied his reins to the rusted metal gate.

She grasped the hilt of her dagger as she stepped over the gate. Weeds and rocks crunched under her boot with each slow step. The silence that hung over the dilapidated church grounds did nothing to ease the restlessness creeping through her thoughts.

Uncertainty settled in the pit of her stomach as she approached the church's rotting wooden door. The familiar sensation of the silver's chill sent shivers down her spine.

She stuck her head through the exposed half of the doorway, using the light streaming in from the holes in the ceiling to see what was waiting inside for her.

The first thing she noticed was the smell. The air reeked of mildew and decay. Most of the pews were left as if nothing had ever happened, though a few of them were upturned or splintered. There were rugs stuffed in the window cavities to limit the amount of light that could stream in. She speculated that it was a means of protection for a vampire returning to the church when dawn lit up the sky with enchanting warm colours. Helena was able to participate in the tournament during the day, Catherine had an inkling that her armour likely protected her undead skin from the sun.

Catherine stepped back and kicked in the door. The door shattered as it hit the ground, stirring up a cloud of dust.

The sudden noise startled some of the bats that found refuge in the darkest corners of the building.

She yelped and covered her head with her arms.

Screeching and flapping destroyed the silence inside the church. The swarm of bats flew out through the openings in the ceiling. Seconds passed and their shrieks became nothing more than faint echoes in the distance.

She lowered her arms when she deemed it safe enough to do so and continued surveying the church.

After seeing the damage that a pair of vampires could do in a fight, terror crept up on Catherine once more and dug its talons into her mind.

She stepped over the door and into the church, immediately feeling a drop in temperature. She assumed that was the lack of sunlight and firelight, though she couldn't be sure.

She took another few steps, staring at the tarnished cross on the back wall.

Catherine had sworn an oath to the king's people and God Himself, but she couldn't help but to feel like an unwelcome outsider in what was once a house of God.

The floor creaked beneath her boots as she crept past the rows of pews.

Her heart pounded so hard in her chest that she could

feel it pulse in her eardrums.

Catherine paused for a moment at the podium where the altar would've been, bringing her face to face with the weathered cross still attached to the wall. She reached for the cross around her neck with her free hand, stroking the cold metal with her thumb before letting it fall back against her tunic.

She looked to her left and found the door that once led to the priest's chambers when this church was still in use. The door itself was so damaged that any rough movement would cause it to fall off its hinges. She walked towards the door, her footsteps echoing around the church. The door's hinges screeched as she gently pushed it open.

The room was dark, musty, and reeked of death.

A lone stone coffin stood in the centre of the room.

She walked around the coffin and stopped at the end, staring down at the lid. Her hands ran down the sides of the lid and stopped at an indentation.

She let out a measured breath to steady herself and adjusted her hold on the stone before she dragged the lid towards her.

It wasn't until the cover was halfway off that Catherine let go. She looked inside, using what little light filtering into the room to discern what she was seeing.

Something was inside. And it wasn't a decaying corpse.

She unsheathed her dagger, waiting for any sign of movement.

She only needed to see tendrils of shining copper hair to

A Knight's Blood

know who had claimed the coffin. A longsword bearing what the sigil of the Knights Templar on its hilt sat within her callused hands and upon a red wool kirtle. Catherine had no idea how she got hold of such a sword, but the serene expression on Helena's face banished any speculation that danced amongst her thoughts.

The woman's lips were luscious and pink. The slightest sliver of her fangs protruded enough to press against her lower lip. The fact she was dressed like a noblewoman did nothing to detract from how defined her shoulders and arms were. She most certainly appeared as if she could heft the two-handed sword she cradled against her body even if she didn't have the supernatural strength that came with undeath.

The knight drew in a deep breath and told herself that she needed two sets of remains in order to secure the choice in who she would be forced to marry.

The chance to complete half of her task was right there.

She held the dagger to Helena's pale throat, her hand shaking as she tried to hold it steady. The longer she stared at the slumbering vampire, the quicker Catherine lost her nerve.

Helena's eyelids snapped open, revealing the same glowing red eyes that haunted Catherine's nightmares. Before Catherine could even gasp, Helena slammed her fist into the knight's elbow hard enough to force the dagger away.

Catherine's yelp echoed around the room as she staggered back from the coffin.

Before Catherine could regain her balance, Helena sat up and pressed the tip of her sword against the knight's chest, keeping Catherine at a distance without hurting her.

Indignance crinkled the lines on her face. She bared her

fangs at Catherine. The skin on the wrist Catherine had slashed earlier was mottled and grey from when the silver dagger scorched her skin.

'Well, isn't that a wonderful way to wake someone who saved your life?' Helena asked with a snarl. Even though she kept herself poised and ready to strike, Helena wanted to be a little snarky. If only to fluster Catherine more. 'Not very honourable of you, is it, Lady Seymour?'

Catherine didn't dare move.

A memory from last night flashed in her mind; a pair of red glowing eyes and gleaming saliva-coated fangs.

'You… you killed him. You killed Sir Alwyn,' Catherine said.

'That was Erik's doing. If it weren't for me knocking you to the ground, he would've killed you too,' Helena replied. 'I saved your life. You could at least be grateful.'

Catherine stepped back, making space between herself and the tip of Helena's blade. She cringed as her bruised back collided with the wall behind her.

'Who is Erik?' she demanded. 'Why is he brawling with you in my village?'

Helena vaulted over the lip of her makeshift bed. She was by Catherine's side in a second. A gleeful smirk spread across her soft lips as she pressed her blade up against Catherine's neck, revelling in how the knight's pulse danced against the metal. She clicked her tongue and shook her head at the woman on the other side of her sword.

The surprise that widened Catherine's eyes filled Helena

with glee. Never in her vampiric life had she found someone so fun to twist around her finger.

'Why would I tell you who he is?' Helena asked. She grasped Catherine's chin with her free hand and tilted the knight's head up towards the ceiling. She ran her tongue across her lips as she saw how furiously Catherine's blood thumped through her veins. 'I don't want you gallivanting into the darkness and getting yourself killed. Unless that's the reason you keep trying to kill me–in which case, I will reluctantly oblige.'

The vampire was inches from her lips and neck, making Catherine's stomach churn with unwelcome yearning. Her hand tightly wound around her dagger's hilt.

'I must protect the people from the likes of you. I will not allow you feast on the innocent as if they were your personal larder! Whether God guides my hand or not, I will protect the people of Birkstead until my dying breath,' Catherine said.

Helena rolled her eyes. She pressed the blade harder against Catherine's neck, cutting into her skin. Blood welled on the edge of the sword. The vampire breathed in deeply, savouring its rich scent. She did her best to ignore how delicious the knight smelled. Helena frowned at Catherine.

'Noble goals often lead to a terrible demise. What happened between me and Erik last night is an example of what happens when humans get involved in vampire politics. You'd best stay out of it,' Helena warned.

Against her better judgement, Catherine snorted.

'It seems as if you aren't very good with vampire politics,' Catherine teased. 'Erik got away.'

With Helena's sword digging into her neck and her

95

shining fangs not too far from the drops of blood that slid down her collarbone, Catherine tried her hardest not to move. She needed to get out of her grasp before Helena decided she was tired of playing games. Catherine held the vampire's gaze as she inched the tip of her dagger towards Helena's ribs, trying to catch her unaware.

Without even blinking, Helena moved her sword away from Catherine's neck and grabbed her wrist. The dagger struck the wall behind Catherine. The impact rung out through the air, echoing around the stone walls with a metallic twang.

A smirk pulled at Helena's lips. The vampire's face was so close to the knight's that they almost touched, leaving only a small distance between their lips. She clicked her tongue and shook her head at Catherine as if she were scolding a misbehaving child.

'I wouldn't do that if I were you. You need me,' Helena teased. 'You stand no chance of being able kill a vampire on your own. No matter how skilled or stealthy you think you are, I'm strong enough and fast enough to outmanoeuvre whatever course of action you take. You mortals have such inflated egos. You overestimate what you're capable of.'

Helena brought her sword to her lips, licking the blood from its edge.

'Are you saying that you'll help me kill Erik?' the knight asked, her voice near breathless.

Helena's sword fell to the ground. It clanged at her feet as she pinned Catherine's shoulder to the wall.

Catherine held her breath.

Helena leant towards her neck with her tongue pressing

against her sharp teeth.

The knight's fear was drowned out by the thrill of feeling her fangs pressing against her skin again.

Helena slammed Catherine's wrist against the stone, sending a jolt of pain through her hand and forcing the dagger to fall from her grasp.

Catherine's heartbeat was so loud she couldn't hear her weapon hit the mossy stone floor. All she could think about was how close Helena was. She noticed the scents other than blood's metallic musk that clung to Helena's body. The vampire's hair smelt of charred wood, smoke from dragon's blood resin, and mead. Catherine's head pounded as all those different smells swirled and overwhelmed her already scattered thoughts.

Helena's tongue touched Catherine's neck, lapping the blood from the fresh wound.

A moan slipped from the knight's lips. No matter how harshly she mentally scolded herself, she couldn't deny that Helena's touch was alluring and utterly intoxicating. Her whole body tensed with anticipation.

Helena paused mid-lick. Her gip on Catherine tightened as another moan rang in her ears like a symphony. She chuckled, pressing her lips against the knight's skin.

She realised she'd left Catherine's question unanswered.

Helena reluctantly pulled her lips away from the weeping wound on her neck and sighed, smirking at Catherine's blissful half-smile and how her eyelids slowly fluttered open.

'Help you kill Erik? That was not what I was suggesting

at all. But, if you wish to play the damsel in distress that I save from Erik's clutches, you're more than welcome to,' Helena teased.

Catherine's smile fell, frowning as she looked the vampire up and down with her eyes narrowed. Her hands balled into fists.

'Very funny. You're delusional if you believe that I'm going to play the damsel in distress,' Catherine replied.

Before she could continue her rebuttal, Helena returned her attention to the wound on the knight's neck, pressing her tongue against the welling blood.

Catherine found herself melting under her touch once again, losing the will to say what was on her mind.

'I know,' Helena cooed. Her tongue flicked across the slit in Catherine's neck. 'I've played that role before and despised every second of it. Noble life only benefits those who get to have a say in their future. I swore to myself that I would never let that happen again.'

The knight's mouth fell open as she realised what Helena alluded to.

The seal of the Knights Templar shone with the intensity of its wielder's crimson eyes.

How could a creature so dark be in possession of an artefact emblazoned with the symbol so closely affiliated to the army of warriors dedicated to the Church?

'How does a former damsel like you end up with a long-sword like that?' Catherine asked, nodding towards the sword that lay abandoned at the vampire's feet.

A Knight's Blood

Helena looked up at her, eyebrow raised.

'You're awfully inquisitive, aren't you?' Helena asked in return. 'My father was a Templar and a fairly wealthy nobleman. I stole it from him when I ran away from home. It's the only thing I kept from my life before I reawakened. It's a reminder of where I came from and who I don't want to become.'

'Were you close to him?' Catherine asked, barely keeping her curiosity at bay.

Helena's nails dug into her shoulder, giving a silent warning.

Catherine clenched her teeth, trying not to react to the sting that followed.

The bridge of Helena's nose crinkled as if she'd tasted something foul.

'No. He was a selfish bastard, obsessed with his own power, and refused to think of anyone but himself. I'm glad he's gone,' Helena seethed. Her gaze returned to Catherine's neck. Her tongue slithered across the knight's jaw and up to her ear lobe. She grinned when Catherine moaned in response. 'I don't want to think about him. All I want, right now, is your blood.'

The suction between Helena's lips and her neck began to turn the skin around it as purple as the bruises upon her back. Every nerve in her body was set alight. Catherine arched her back, pushing her neck closer to Helena's mouth.

'Good girl,' Helena purred. Her words were impeded by the fang that dug into the cut she coaxed blood from.

Despite the fact that her mind screamed at her for allowing herself to remain vulnerable, the pleasure that made her entire body tingle kept her rooted to the spot.

Helena's fangs sunk into Catherine's neck, forcing a delighted cry from Catherine's lips as more blood welled onto Helena's tongue.

'Wait, won't biting me turn me into a vampire?' Catherine asked, her eyes suddenly wide. If Helena were to confirm that was the case, then she'd started the path to becoming undead in the manor chapel. 'I mean, does getting bitten any time before death make me like you?'

The knight immediately thought back to the night before and mentally scolded herself for letting her panic forget the fact she did indeed know how vampires were reawakened. After all, she attempted to behead Walter's corpse because there was a chance he would become a vampire too.

The vampire pulled her fangs out from her neck and laughed at Catherine's ignorance. Helena twirled the bottom of the knight's braid around her fingers, revelling in the softness of her dark hair. Helena gave a little shake of her head, her tongue darting out of her lips to lick up some of the blood that coated her mouth.

'That's sweet,' Helena replied, forcing her bottom lip to protrude in a playful pout. 'No, that's not how that works. I'm sure there's more ways to do so but I'm only aware of two ways to become a vampire. The first is the most common. A vampire will drain a mortal of blood and have said mortal drink some vampiric blood in return before they die. Then, they spend anywhere from one to four days in a comatose state, only to reawaken as a vampire when the process is complete.'

Catherine let out a sigh of relief. She wasn't going to become a vampire. But she couldn't deny the fact that she wanted

to know what else could transform her into a member of the undead. She'd only known about the one. 'What's the other way?'

'Curious, aren't you?' Helena asked. 'It's near impossible to achieve, but someone would have to have done it before
or there wouldn't be vampires today. You'd have to seek out the
sídhe and make a deal with them for power and immortality. Any
way it happens, a lot of vampiric powers and weaknesses remain
the same. You will have bloodthirst, weakness to silver, hawthorn, and yew, as well as having an increased sensitivity to the
sun. Sunlight can kill you if you stay out in it without wearing
protection for too long.'

'The sídhe?'

Helena let Catherine's braid fall against her chest as
she busied her hands with the underside of the knight's jaw. She
lowered her head and ran her tongue across the blood that welled
on Catherine's neck, humming with delight as the taste of copper
danced upon what was left of her tastebuds.

'Oh, right. You English call them something different. I
believe you refer to them as the fae, faeries, or fair folk?' Helena
explained. 'They're powerful beings that enjoy playing tricks on
mortals too stupid to see their manipulations for what they are.
It's the reason why vampires can glamour themselves much like
the sídhe can. They gave us that power among others. It's magic
that allows us vampires to function the way we do.'

'Have you ever met one?'

'No, and I don't think I will. They're fairly secretive,'
Helena replied. 'Though I am curious as to how you were able
to see through the glamour I was putting on in the tent after the
tournament. How did you do it?'

Shivers ran through Catherine's body as her skin tingled when Helena ran her fingers across her neck. She stared into the vampire's eyes as she tried to shrug.

'I don't know. I just can,' Catherine replied. 'My necklace also gets incredibly cold around vampires. I have no clue why.'

The vampire tenderly licked the wound again, coaxing another breathy moan from the knight. She smiled against her neck, revelling in the sound of Catherine slowly losing herself to those little moments of pleasure.

'Usually only the sídhe, witches, or other vampires can see through our glamours… Are you a witch?'

Catherine's eyes opened wide and she stuttered in shock at the vampire's question. 'I most certainly am not a witch!'

'Interesting,' Helena said. 'There's nothing wrong with being a witch, by the way. The Church are scared of people with power they cannot explain. But the fact that you can see through glamours without having power is very intriguing. Between this and tasting like heaven, you're proving to be a unique find.'

The way in which Helena stroked the sensitive skin underneath her ear with her fingertip forced her body to relax. Catherine's thoughts continued their panicked descent, filling her mind with muddled emotions and uncertainty. She knew she shouldn't be so vulnerable with the undead woman that gently lapped her blood, and yet, there was something comforting about Helena and her playful wisdom.

Her breath stopped in her throat as Helena licked Catherine's blood off her lips and stared down at the knight with a wry smile. She couldn't help but to lean closer towards Helena's face

A Knight's Blood

when the copper-haired vampire pursed her lips and raised an eyebrow at her. The chill emanating from her necklace did little to distract her. The heat in her cheeks and belly served to chase away some of the cold that coaxed goosebumps onto her chest.

She sighed in disappointment as Helena pulled away, grinning.

Helena lowered her head and returned her lips to Catherine's neck, gingerly lapping at the wound. The vampire loosened her grip on the knight as she drank, careful not to drain too much blood and leave Catherine too weak to return home. She licked the bitemarks and pulled away from Catherine's soft skin, pouting because she wanted more.

'No one ever taught us vampires were masters in the arts of seduction,' Catherine muttered, chuckling at her own joke as both lust and loss of blood made her dizzy.

'Perhaps they should teach you how to protect yourselves against those with charisma?' Helena replied, her tone equally as playful as Catherine's. 'After all, mortals should know better than to allow a dangerous creature to play with them. If their lives are not taken, their blood will be.'

'If they don't invite said creatures into their bed, that is. As if bedding a vampire would be the thing to ruin a man's reputation,' Catherine jested. The smile that stretched across her face faded as she realised what would happen if she had behaved the way her colleagues did. She shied away from Helena and frowned at her own feet, suddenly ashamed of herself. 'It wouldn't ruin theirs but it would ruin mine. It wouldn't even be the fact that I bedded a vampire that would do so, but rather the fact that I bedded someone that wasn't the husband I'm expected to take. The very fact that I refuse to take a husband in the first place causes my father much grief because I refuse to do as he asks. In the end, I may not even have a choice in my own future.'

The mischievous glint in Helena's gaze remained, even if the smirk she wore fell from her lips. She ran her fingers down Catherine's cheek again and pouted playfully.

'That's the game men play. It's how they force us to obey their every demand. God, Church, king, lord; it doesn't matter who does the demanding, they only wish for their requests be fulfilled exactly to their liking. You're already pushing the limits of what they will give you; they won't like letting you have more,' Helena said. 'Power and control are things they do not wish for anyone other than themselves to wield. Don't fall for the trap they've laid for you. You're better than that.'

The knight's next breath shook in her chest as echoes of her father's words disrupted her already chaotic thoughts. A frown touched her face, remembering how many times he called her entitled and ungrateful for the life he was going to force her to follow. She attempted to keep her emotions from showing upon her face, but the way in which she clenched her jaw and her fists ruined those attempts within seconds.

Years of being told she was never good enough to step up and take over her father's position on her own weighed heavy. She tried to parse how this vampire saw the worth in her that her father didn't and was still mystified by it.

'How do you know?' Catherine asked, her head shaking slightly with disbelief.

Helena's expression softened to something sorrowful and empathetic. Her eyes seemed distant, lost in thought. Rage and sorrow swirled within her crimson irises as her biceps stiffened.

'My parents told me day after day that I was only worth who I married. I believed them for the longest time until I finally realised that they wanted what was best for them, and not for me. Nobles will always want power and prestige, that much hasn't changed since I left that life behind. Everyone deserves better than being forced to marry for anything other than love.'

Catherine noticed that Helena was adept at changing her tone and body language to suit her needs, but she seemed to be telling the truth.

'Some people don't have the luxury of doing that. In my case, I have a duty to the people of Birkstead. They deserve to have stability and safety without wondering how much they'll have to pay for it,' she replied.

'Is sacrificing your happiness worth it? What about sacrificing your dreams and everything you've worked for?' the vampire asked. 'There will always be a way to help them without dooming yourself to a life you despise.'

Catherine had no response to that. She stayed silent, hoping that she didn't have to answer. She had no idea how she'd even start.

'I see,' Helena said with a sigh. She stepped aside, picking up her sword and draping it across her shoulders. She put her weight all on one hip and nodded towards the door.

'You might want to head home soon. Your father will want to introduce you to some new suitors,' Helena said.

'Helena…' Catherine started. Her voice trailed off as she lost track of what she wanted to say as she watched the vampire climb back into the coffin she'd claimed as her bed.

Unsure of how to respond to the vampire's cold

shoulder, Catherine picked up her dagger and slipped it into its sheath before she marched out of the room, stopping to glance over her shoulder at the cross upon the wall. She hoped doing so would bring her some peace, but all it did was overcomplicate what had just occurred.

Her thoughts bounced between going back to Helena and attempting to find and kill the vampire called Erik. Above all, she had to ensure the people's protection. It was her knightly duty to do so.

The vampire's words echoed, forcing her to think about whether sacrificing her happiness and goals were worth becoming some nobleman's wife in order to potentially get the chance to help the people.

Unable to make up her mind, Catherine untied Smokey's reins from the gate. She mounted her horse and urged him back towards Birkstead, hoping to clear her head in the village square before she went home.

12

The evening air ran its icy hands down Catherine's spine as Smokey trotted down Birkstead's main road.

His hooves kicked up dirt and dust as his rider oversaw the villagers preparing to turn in for the night.

Flames crackled in fireplaces visible from open windows, flickering underneath pots filled with various vegetables for dinner. The smell of simple cooking filled Catherine's nose as she passed the stone buildings.

The fresh air served to dispel the dizziness she experienced before. Though she hadn't stopped thinking about what happened with Helena. Her necklace rubbed up against the scab covering Helena's bite. The friction helped relieve some of the itchiness, but didn't stop it completely.

She nodded to the villagers who acknowledged her as she passed, a warm smile upon her lips. She waved at some of the children who stopped to gape at the sword and dagger upon her hip and the horse she rode.

The children immediately brightened and waved back. Some stared with eyes so wide that stars could call their pupils home. Their toothy grins made Catherine smile all the wider. She was sure some of the little girls that saw her realised they could become a warrior like the boys wanted. Her heart swelled with happiness.

Moments like this made the blood, sweat, and tears

Catherine put into her training worth it. She hoped that, one day, those little girls would grow up to inspire others just as she hoped she inspired them.

Dusk's orange glow settled over all of the thatched roofs in front of her, glinting in the stained glass remaining in the windows of the newly ruined village chapel. Whenever the glare shined on her face, she narrowed her eyes to try and see through the blinding light.

The villagers that worked to clear the debris from the chapel put down brooms and buckets when they noticed the sunset. Some swiped their foreheads with their sleeves to collect the sweat from a hard day's work.

A man in a dirty tunic and a straw hat that looked like a bucket called for the workers to head home.

Catherine slowed her horse to a walk and then stopped beside him, smiling down at the man she assumed to be the foreman.

'How goes the clean up?' she asked.

'Ah, Lady Seymour. Tis good to see you,' he called as he brushed his dust-covered hands onto his tunic. 'We're making good progress. Broken glass was the first thing we cleared. Tomorrow we'll be salvaging what furniture we can. I hope whatever we can't salvage can either be repaired or turned into something new.'

'It sounds like you've been making progress. I'll come down tomorrow to help with the furniture. I'll also sneak down a treat or two,' she said, giving him a conspiratorial wink. 'I'm sure the kitchen staff could spare some sweets.'

He beamed and gave her a small bow. 'Thank you, my

lady. Your kindness is appreciated.'

'I hope that the night treats you all well,' Catherine said and gave him a parting nod.

As she was about to spur Smokey onward, his ears flattened against his head and refused to move.

She looked in the direction that caught Smokey's attention and straightened up in her saddle.

Two men clad in worn leather and armed to the teeth strode down the village's main road. The pair appeared to be the type of mercenaries that floated into villages and towns in search of vampires, or peasants with teeth sharp enough to pass as vampiric. Sometimes it didn't even matter what their teeth looked like, they could pull the teeth from dogs or wolves and the Church would be none the wiser to the deception.

It didn't surprise Catherine that mercenaries would appear in the village. News of the chapel's destruction spread through Birkstead's ranks like wildfire. From the reports she'd heard from the other knights, these two were the first mercenaries to visit Birkstead in over four months. Other mercenaries didn't think to use any of the people in Birkstead as props for a scam, but since word had spread of vampires in Birkstead, that would no longer be the case.

Catherine dismounted from Smokey's back and tied his reins to the nearest post so he wouldn't run away should a fight occur. He had been trained to behave calmly in combat situations, but Catherine didn't want to take any chances. She really didn't want to walk back to the manor should Smokey run away.

The loudest of the two was tall, had hair like straw, and a

beard so scraggly he appeared as if he rarely bothered to bathe. A few teeth were missing and a few more were rotten. His pants were covered in mud.

The other man was at least a head taller than his companion. He had brown hair pulled into two braids that kept his locks out of his eyes. A large that ran across his face.

The two mercenaries marched down the road, ignoring the villagers that stopped and turned to walk away as soon as they saw the rugged pair of mercenaries. The shorter blond pointed some of the fleeing villagers out to his companion. They laughed at their fear, relishing in the small amount of chaos they were able to sow with very little effort.

Catherine's jaw tightened. She watched them walk towards a group of teenagers too engrossed in their conversation to notice them. She placed her hand on the hilt of her blade as she made her way towards the group of chattering girls. By the time she'd walked close enough to hear the girls' laughter, she noticed that the two men stood not far from the group, watching the four girls with grimy, sly smiles.

The scruffy blond leant towards his companion and whispered something, the pair eyeing the brunette in a faded green kirtle.

The girl's smile was wide and radiant. She placed her hand on a friend's shoulder as she laughed at her joke, completely unaware of the danger they were in.

The two men looked at each other and nodded in agreement. They reached for their swords, stalking closer to the girls.

Rage slithered through Catherine's veins. She gritted her teeth and unsheathed her sword. The knight stood in front of the girls, flourishing her sword and pointing the tip at the mercenaries. The corner of Catherine's lip curled to reveal her best snarl.

A part of her wished she had Helena's razor-sharp fangs.

'Don't even think about touching them,' Catherine said.

The girls behind the knight bunched together, grasping each other's arms. Their eyes were wide and their mouths were agape in fear and confusion.

Both mercenaries glanced at the sword, then at Catherine.

The brown-haired man glared at her with distaste.

The blond smirked at the tip of her blade.

'Such hostility. We only wanted to talk with those lovely ladies behind you,' the blond said.

Catherine's skin crawled. His sinister smirk made her want to slap the amusement right off his pockmarked face.

'Not while I'm here you won't,' Catherine replied.

The stocky man nodded walked towards the girls. He dodged Catherine's swipe and grabbed the brunette in green, dragging her away from her friends as she screamed.

The group screamed and reached for their friend before she was pulled close to the mercenary's chest.

He grabbed her mouth mid-yelp and inspected her teeth closely, his own teeth on show as he grinned. 'My, what fangs you have, my dear,' he sneered. 'I think the Church will like these.'

Catherine glanced at the girl, noting her lack of red irises and the absence of the tell-tale chill that accompanied the presence of vampires. It was just as she thought. They were a pair of cowards looking to exploit the bounty on vampiric remains.

'Let her go,' Catherine commanded. 'That girl is not a vampire.'

The girl in green squirmed against the mercenary's grasp, squealing as she realised what could potentially happen to her. Tears welled in her eyes. She pleaded to be let go, her voice phlegmy.

The straw-haired man looked Catherine up and down. He snorted and shook his head. He roughly grabbed the girl's chin and wiggled her jaw, grinning wider when he saw the rage building upon the knight's face.

'The Church doesn't care how they get a set of ashes and sharp teeth, they're happy to pay it. And they'll pay us a pretty penny for teeth like hers.'

'Girls, go to safety. I'll handle this,' Catherine said, turning her head to look at the trio behind her.

The three girls looked up at Catherine and gave her hurried nods. They scurried towards the villagers congregated around the chapel. The group of people embraced them and formed a protective semi-circle around them, watching in horror as one of their own remained in the mercenaries' clutches.

The blond mercenary chuckled. 'And how would a harlot with a sword handle us?'

Her braids whipped behind her as she turned back to face the smarmy man. The want, no, the need to wipe that smirk off his face overtook the logical side of her brain that only wanted to spook them into letting the girl go. If she did manage to scare them off, who was to say that they wouldn't come back? That couldn't happen.

With a flick of her wrist, the tip of Catherine's blade sliced through the blond's cheek as easily as if she had done the same to a length of silk. She raised an eyebrow at them and swished the tip of her sword from side to side, pointing at each of them and daring them to react.

The smirk fell right from the blond's face. Blood trickled down his pocked cheek. He touched his face and stared at the blood on his fingertips. He showed it to his companion before glancing down at it again, frowning.

'That bitch cut me,' he complained.

Catherine pulled her dagger from her belt, holding it in such a way that any other knight would've cringed. She flung it at the brown-haired mercenary and it hit its mark, sinking into his shoulder.

He yelped in pain, folding over as he winced and groaned. He loosened his hold on the girl to yank the dagger out, blood slickening his glove. The scar on his face warped as he grimaced.

The girl in green took advantage of the distraction and wrestled her way out of his weakened grasp, pushing with all of her might. She broke free and fled towards the group of villagers, tears streaming down her face as the man in the straw hat embraced her in a tight hug.

Catherine smiled as she heard loud exclaims of relief, though the girl's sobs broke her heart.

Though the girl was rightfully shaken, she was safe. That

was all Catherine cared about. Now, she could give these two mercenaries Hell.

She glared at the pair, preparing for a proper fight.

The taller mercenary stumbled and finally yanked the dagger free from his shoulder, grumbling as more blood darkened his clothes. He grunted and threw the dagger to the ground. He clenched his teeth and bared them at the knight, pulling his sword out of its sheath.

The blond reached for a sword with a huff. His nostrils flared. 'You're going to regret that.'

The brown-haired mercenary spat a glob of mucus at her feet.

'To fight me is to offend House Seymour. My father may not demand blood, but I damn well do. Do you dare incur my wrath?' Catherine asked.

The blond tossed his head, giving his companion the signal to act.

Catherine and flourished her sword, sneering down her nose at the two of them.

The brown-haired mercenary charged towards her with his weapon raised high. His bloodshot eyes were wide and wild with fury.

Her sword clashed with his, sliding the edge of her weapon down to his hilt and locking it in place. She pushed his elbow, along with his sword, down to create an opening. Before he could react, she whipped her sword around and plunged it through his chest.

He screamed as she slid the blade in further, pushing

through layers of leather.

Catherine kept her sword embedded in him for a moment, glaring at him with the corner of her lip twitching into a sneer. She let go of the man's elbow and yanked her sword out of his chest with an awful squelch. Her blood-slickened sword gleamed in the dying light. She adjusted her grip on her blade, wielding it as an assassin would their dagger. She spun out and swung her sword in an arc, catching the mercenary's throat with the edge.

Catherine readjusted her stance, holding her weapon properly once more.

A line of red trickled down his neck like a string of rubies. He grasped his throat, attempting to keep the wound closed with his already bloodied hand. He coughed blood as he stumbled forward, sword raised again.

Catherine stepped out of his way and brought her pommel down on the back of his head. A sickening crack echoed.

The mercenary collapsed to the ground, emitting unholy gurgling groans as blood began pooling underneath his body.

She crossed the splattered ground to pick up her dagger. With her dagger in one hand and her sword in the other, she turned to face the blond staring at her. She slammed the heel of her boot on the brown-haired man's hand, forcing his hand to splay over his sword. Catherine didn't break eye-contact with the remaining mercenary, twisting her heel on his hand for good measure. The knight walked away from the dying man, cocking her head with a quirk of her eyebrow.

Catherine knew that she was being unnecessarily harsh,

but she was out of patience for anyone that preyed on her people. She needed to send a message.

'You didn't make me regret anything. Like I said, this village is under the protection of House Seymour. If you have a problem with that, you can leave. Or you can end up like him,' Catherine announced, pointing at the man she left to bleed out on the village road with her sword. 'It's your choice.'

He glanced between the knight and his dying companion. The blond slowly lowered his sword. His gaze lingered on the other mercenary as he wondered if fighting her was even worth it. His sword whined as he slid it back into its sheath.

'Smart,' Catherine said. Fury and satisfaction danced through her thoughts. 'If you're so desperate for the bounty that you'd kidnap someone, you have a body right here you can pull the teeth from and burn. You might want to smell posies when you're done, burning flesh smells worse than death.'

The blond side-eyed her. He knelt down beside his companion's corpse, annoyance pinching his features.

She sheathed her weapons and retrieved Smokey, who remained where she'd tied him. She led him over to the villagers outside the church, leaving the mercenary to decide whether he would take the body with him or not.

The villagers looked at her with wide eyes, unsure how to react. Women clutched small children close to their bodies, preparing to flee should the mercenary turn on them.

'I'm sorry you had to see that,' Catherine said.

The girl the mercenaries attempted to abduct wove her way through the crowd and stood where she could see Catherine face to face. She grasped her dress and smiled at the knight, tears still streaming down her cheeks.

Her throat tightened when she saw that fear caused the girl's arms to tremble. She wanted to reach out and pull her into a hug, but had a feeling that getting blood on her might make things worse.

'Are you alright?' Catherine asked.

The girl sniffled. The whites of her eyes were pink and glassy, no doubt from sobbing as hard as she had. She nodded slowly. 'I thought I was as good as dead,' she replied.

'I wouldn't let them hurt you,' Catherine said. 'Do you have someone who can look after you?'

'Yes, my lady. Mamma and papa will be back from tending the sheep soon,' she replied, her voice breaking as she continued sniffing back tears.

Catherine glanced over her shoulder and noticed that both mercenaries were no longer where she'd left them. Unease settled in the back of her mind, though it could've just been adrenaline leaving her body.

'Though I believe the remaining man shouldn't bother you anymore, I want to stay until the night patrol gets here, just in case. I will be petitioning my father for patrols during the day so this doesn't happen again,' Catherine announced to the crowd. She turned to the girl before her and smiled warmly once more. 'Is there someone you can stay with until your parents return from the field? I'd rather you be able to quickly find safety with others if that coward decides to come back.'

The foreman stepped through the crowd, still holding his straw hat. 'My lads and I are more than happy to look after her until her parents get back.'

One of the girl's friends placed her hand on her shoulder and smiled. 'We'll also stay with her.'

Catherine's smile widened as she surveyed the crowd. The many faces that watched her differed in age, appearance, and occupation. There was something so wonderful about how they were more than willing to look out for this girl as if she were their sister or daughter. She couldn't bite back the sadness that accompanied that sense of wonder.

Perhaps they wouldn't need to rely on each other for safety if more was done to ensure their peace.

If she were able to run Birkstead, she'd do so many things differently. However, she might never get the chance to do so.

13

Catherine's soft blue kirtle danced against her legs as she moved. She walked into her father's study without knocking, her head held high. Her father had demanded to see her once again and she was obligated to do as he wished, lest he make life even more unpleasant. That didn't mean she couldn't make his life unpleasant in return. It seemed only fair.

Her worries regarding the mercenaries in Birkstead remained firmly in her thoughts, even as she bid Aldric and Robert farewell when they began their patrol. The two of them could more than handle the scruffy blond if he returned for revenge.

'A pair of mercenaries attempted to kidnap a girl a few hours ago,' Catherine said. 'Thankfully, I was passing through Birkstead in time to stop them. Word has spread about vampires in our area and those looking to make money by any means necessary are looking to take advantage of that. I insist we have knights in the village during the day as well as keeping the nightly rounds in place.'

Lord Seymour looked up from the letter he was writing and stared at his daughter. As soon as he saw her indignant expression, he glanced back down at his paper and finished his sentence with a flourish of his quill. He put his quill down and threaded his fingers together as he leant on his elbows.

'Very well,' Geoffrey said with a sigh. 'Consider it done.'

Instead of feeling the relief she expected, she only found herself growing increasingly wary. Catherine narrowed her eyes at her father, pursing her lips in silence. She didn't trust his demeanour one bit. She had to fight him tooth and nail for everything, yet he agreed to this demand without a fight.

'Just like that?' she asked, raising an eyebrow.

Geoffrey stared at her. Annoyance weighed heavy on his aging face. 'I received reports from nearby lords that they've been having similar issues. Best to stay on top of these matters lest they get out of hand.'

Though it was sound logic, she was still suspicious of her father's motivations.

'That aside, what did you wish to speak to me about?' she asked.

'I'm sure you're well aware that the first twenty-four hours of your vampire hunt are coming to a close, so I won't remind you of the time you have left to complete your task,' Geoffrey replied. 'I called you here to talk about your mentor's funeral.'

'Oh,' was all Catherine could muster in reply.

'His body is currently being prepared for burial. The funeral is in two days from now. We'll be hosting his family for a small ceremony in the manor chapel,' Geoffrey said. 'I know he was well loved by Birkstead's community, but I don't want commonfolk in the manor. I invited the sons of my friends overseas to join us for the event. Some of them are very intrigued to meet you.'

And there it was. The real reason why he was so quick

to accept her demand.

Catherine clenched her teeth and gripped her sword tight for a second, releasing it moments later. She kept her hand on the hilt to keep herself grounded. The end of her braid slapped her cheek as she shook her head at Geoffrey.

'You said you'd give me a week, I have six days left,' Catherine snapped.

She went to continue speaking, but stopped with her mouth hanging open. Her chest grew colder the longer she stood. Hand still laying lazily on her sword's hilt, she widened her stance. 'Something's wrong.'

Screams erupted from outside Geoffrey's study.

Nostrils flaring, she swung around to face the door and drew her sword. Catherine kept her gaze on the door. The knight slowly stalked her way towards the screams.

'What was that?' Geoffrey asked, looking around frantically.

'A vampire,' Catherine muttered in reply.

She ignored her father's panic and leant against the doorframe. The folds of her dress brushed over her blade's bare edges, fraying where the sword sliced through the threads. She pressed her hand on the wooden door, drawing in a deep breath. She opened the door, prepared to face whatever threat waited for her head on.

Or so she thought.

Her ferocity cracked as she saw the familiar burly figure of Sir Alwyn plunging his fangs into a woman's neck.

The few clothes that covered his body were torn and dirty, as if he'd broken through the dungeon walls with nothing but his bare hands. Walter's nails were cracked and covered in gore. Blood trickled down his chin and onto his chest. His eyes were wide, bloodshot, and frenzied.

This was what the Church toted as the picture of a vampire. And what she saw before her scared Catherine down to her core.

A crowd gathered in the hallway, staring in shock like a herd of deer waiting to see who the hunter would go for next. The servants were ready to sprint down the hall at a moment's notice. Some stepped back slowly, attempting to sneak away without alerting the monster to their movement.

Among those frozen in fear was a copper haired woman in red and a blond man in a fine brown tunic with steel beads in his scraggly hair, glaring at each other. Out of everyone, the aforementioned pair were the only two who didn't move. And they were the only members of the crowd with eyes as red as Walter's had become.

Catherine realised these two they were Helena and Erik, the vampire she was feuding with the night Walter was killed.

The dead knight's hands were covered in viscera up to his elbows, highlighting the bright purple veins popping through his papery skin. He was sickly pale and his irises flashed a dangerous crimson. The fangs protruding from his gums were long and sharp.

Horror leeched the breath from her lungs. Her chest ached. Tears obscured her vision.

The man she'd looked up to and loved as a father was now a creature of death and destruction. And it was her duty to ensure he didn't cause that death and destruction.

Catherine bit back the sobs building in her chest.

She knew what she had to do. This wasn't Walter. Not anymore.

She stepped out of the doorway. Catherine adjusted her stance and her grip on her blade. Two tears slid down her cheek as she tilted her head down and flourished her sword, using the firelight flashing off the steel to catch his attention.

The monster that wore Walter's skin dropped the woman and turned his attention towards Catherine, his chin glistening with his victim's blood.

The woman crawled away before she found her feet and ran, trailing blood along the floor and clamping her hand over her wound.

Some of the servants who were more conscious of the situation followed close behind and shut the door, barricading it with a table to ensure they had time to flee if the vampire returned to attack someone else.

The newly awoken vampire licked the glistening blood from his lips and hungrily glared at Catherine. It was clear the Walter she knew and loved was gone; all that remained was an unbridled craving for the blood splattered all over his skin.

Just from watching him for a few seconds, it seemed as if he didn't remember anything. There was no recognition behind his eyes. His movements were far from the fluid and precise motions he'd use during even the most playful of scraps. All he cared about was satisfying his craving.

Catherine held her sword steady and lunged forward.

She slashed at him, forcing him back as she carved space for herself. Her blade cut through his flesh like butter, her sword's edge gleaming with blood. She feinted to the right with another strike and stepped sideways, ensuring that she wouldn't be cornered.

She struck him again, slicing his chest. The wound bled as if he were mortal, but did nothing to slow him down. He winced when the blade split his skin, but that was his only reaction.

Walter watched her intently, turning with her as she circled him. Spittle and blood flew from his mouth as he bared his fangs and hissed at her. He stalked towards her at the same pace a sparring opponent would, slow and careful, proving to Catherine that he didn't know fast his vampiric nature would allow him to move.

He lunged at her with his arms out and teeth bared.

She swung her sword upward and stepped out of his reach, just as he'd taught her during her training. Her sword cut through his forearm and part of the bone underneath.

Catherine tried not to let her sorrow and bewilderment get the best of her; this was her first real fight to the death with a vampire.

She stared him down, determined to prove she had what it took to be more than a mere noblewoman.

The vampire lunged again.

Her reaction came a second too slow.

Walter dug his claws into her wrist, sending pain shooting through her forearm.

Catherine yelped as his claws dug into her flesh again

and tore through her sleeves, her blood staining the fabric burgundy.

Before he could pull her closer and properly attack her, she swung for his injured wrist. Her sword cleaved straight through muscle and chipped bone. She kicked him square in the chest and knocked him off balance, taking the chance to move across the room to give herself the space to fight.

The severed hand fell from her arm.

She kept her sword out in front of her, never taking her eyes off Walter. Her heart beat like it was going to burst through her ribs. Heavy breaths fell from her mouth as she waited for him to attack again. Fear, sorrow, and guilt forced her fatigued body to tremble, even as she forced her blade to remain steady.

Walter stared at the bloody stump in wonder. The veins in his forehead bulged. He glared at the woman who'd removed his hand, his brows lowering. His face crinkled with rage. He let out another hiss and charged at her, this time faster than any human could muster.

Before she could react, he grasped her neck with his remaining hand, digging his claws into her skin and lifting her off the ground. She kicked at Walter as he attempted to crush her windpipe.

Panic flooded through her mind. Her knuckles turned white from gripping her sword too tight. Her lungs screamed for air. Darkness threatened to eclipse her vision.

Frantic, she swung the blade in an arc towards his neck.

Walter's unnaturally crimson eyes widened as the edge caught midway through his spine.

She yanked the sword out and struck again and again,

hacking away at his spine to ensure that he was rendered use-less, if not finally dead. Her eyes welled with tears and her lungs burnt, but she kept swinging. Her survival depended on it.

The sound of her sword striking bone and cleaving through muscle made her stomach twist. If her throat wasn't already blocked by Walter's hand, it might've been phlegm that blocked it. The next swing was the one that cut through his neck, severing his head from his body.

Walter's head fell off his shoulders, bounced off the floor and rolled, coming to a stop near Erik's feet.

The hand around her throat loosened the moment his spine was no longer attached to his skull.

Walter's headless corpse fell backward, hitting the floor with a wet slap.

Catherine's sword clattered to the ground. She fell to her knees, gasping for air. Her chest heaved with painful, shallow breaths. Her hands slid forward ever so slowly, the blood she landed in slickening her palms and the stone floors.

She'd emerged victorious, but felt as if she'd been dealt the biggest blow imaginable.

Tears fell from her eyes and dampened her sweaty face. Her throat felt as if it had been run over by a carriage. Every breath burned. She lifted her tear-stained face to see the corpse of her mentor, beheaded. She didn't have the strength to do so when Erik killed him and so she had to do so tonight as penance.

The people who had fled from the undead knight crept back into the atrium, curious as to what happened and why there were broken sobs bouncing around the stone walls.

The lord's study door creaked open as Geoffrey emerged

from the doorway, eyes darting around in fear.

'It's safe, my lord,' a servant cowering in the corner called. 'Lady Seymour has dispatched the creature.'

Geoffrey pushed past his door and gasped when he saw his daughter sobbing on the ground, covered in blood. He staggered backward as he took in the caught sight of the headless corpse not far from Catherine. He locked eyes with the nobles and servants congregated at the back of the room. He straightened himself up, clearing his throat to properly compose himself.

Geoffrey marched over to Catherine. Without any compassion or empathy, he placed his hand on her back and leant down towards her ear. 'Get up.'

With her eyes full of tears and her body shaking from exertion and rage, she turned her head slowly towards her father and glared at him. Though her eyes were glassy and bloodshot, her gaze was dangerous.

Geoffrey straightened up and took a few steps back, allowing his daughter to pick up her sword without being in range of its edge.

Her blade sang against stone as she dragged it towards herself. She dug the point into the floor and used it as a crutch to push herself to her feet. Catherine swayed a little, but regained her balance. She stared at her mentor's severed head, trying to keep herself composed.

If only she'd beheaded him in Birkstead, he wouldn't have come back as a vampire, even if someone turned him into one.

'Get the fangs and burn the body,' Geoffrey ordered the servants. 'Make sure you collect the ashes. The Church wants both.'

A young stable boy nodded. He walked over to the head and picked it up, carrying it into the manor's chapel where he could remove the fangs and burn the body whilst not losing any ash to the wind.

Geoffrey turned towards the crowd and smiled widely at them, holding his hands out as if he were proclaiming something to a crowd much larger than the dozen people in front of him.

'My people, the threat has been dealt with. It will be properly destroyed and won't harm any of you again. Servants, it is safe to go back to your duties. If you need to get your wounds checked, please go see the healer. The kitchens will be offering a glass of mead to any nobles who need to steady their nerves,' he announced.

Sighs of relief echoed around the room. People began to chatter amongst themselves as if nothing had happened.

They scattered, walking in small groups down different hallways as if a newly-awakened vampire hadn't caused havoc only moments ago.

Catherine watched them file out, unsure of what she should do or how she should feel. She slid her sword back into its sheath and watched the onlookers leave, scouring the dispersing crowd for Helena. Much to her dismay, she couldn't find her anywhere. She'd lost sight of Erik, too. Catherine sighed and pulled her skirts away from the blood coating her legs, wishing the fabric would stop sticking to her body.

She continued to survey the crowd, desperately fighting against her tiring body to find the pair of vampires that were hiding amongst the humans who believed they were safe once more.

Her tensed shoulders fell in disappointment as the last of the nobles left the atrium and the doors closed behind them. Despite her inability to find the vampires, the cross upon her neck refused to alleviate its icy grasp upon her flesh.

'Excuse me, my lady,' an unfamiliar voice said. His words had a cadence typical of the Danish.

Catherine whipped her head around to face the person behind her as his hand reached out to grasp hers. The breath she was going to release stopped in the base of her throat when she saw his face, focusing immediately on his eyes.

His irises were red.

'I wanted to thank you for your bravery,' he continued, flashing her a fanged smile. 'We'd all be dead if it weren't for you.'

The vampire's braided blond hair fell over the sides of his face, his locks adorned with golden rings and beads. He seemed to be a head taller than Helena and shoulders broader than Aldric's. The way in which he held himself reminded Catherine of a warrior lazing with his comrades after a victorious battle. There was no doubt in her mind that this was the vampire who killed and reawakened Walter, forcing her to kill the very man she saw as a father.

Her hand tightened around the hilt of her sword as she gave him a small sad smile in return. The memory of Helena's explanation of glamours hung in the forefront of her mind, reminding her that he didn't know she could see through his illusions. She swallowed the saliva that coated her tongue and dipped her head a little, feigning embarrassment.

'I don't need thanks,' Catherine replied. 'It is my duty

129

to protect the people from danger.'

She glanced over the vampire's shoulder, catching Geoffrey's lingering gaze and slight smile. She narrowed her eyes at her father, frowning at the way the vampire's hand grasped hers. The knight's upper lip twitched as she turned her attention back to the man still touching her.

As difficult as it was, she kept her sword in its sheath. The chance to claim another set of remains was upon her, but remembered the damage he caused the night he reawakened Walter. She could catch him by surprise, but a vampire could easily overpower any human, let alone a human exhausted from combat. No matter how much she hated to do so, behaving as if he were simply a visiting nobleman was her best option for the time being.

Catherine announced, pointedly tilting her chin in Geoffrey's direction as she dropped the vampire's hand.

Instead of humiliating her father by outing how obviously he wanted to control her life, Geoffrey perked up a little and strode over. The grin he wore upon his face chased away any remnants of the fear he'd faced before.

The vampire chuckled, smirking so much that it switched from flirtatious to sinister quicker than she could blink. 'Given your performance in the tournament and tonight, I'd be surprised if your father didn't get an inundation of interested noblemen in the next few days.'

Geoffrey beamed and patted Catherine on the shoulder, putting on his best imitation of a proud parent. 'You're too kind, Lord—'

'Please, just call me Erik,' the vampire said, answering

Geoffrey's question.

The knight forced a bigger smile to her lips. Panic surged through her thoughts, preventing her from piecing together a logical plan to dispatch Erik. She needed help and rest, both of which were in short supply.

'Very well. It's a pleasure to meet you, Erik,' Geoffrey replied, moving his hand off Catherine's shoulder as he caught sight of how she glared at him. The lord stepped away from his daughter and held his arm out towards his study. 'Come, we'll leave Catherine to visit the healer while we get to know one another over wine and cheese.'

The blond vampire turned to Geoffrey, grinning at Lord Seymour's hospitality. 'That sounds delightful, my lord. I would love to join you,' Erik replied. He glanced over at Catherine. 'I hope you recover quickly, Lady Seymour.'

'Thank you,' Catherine said, bowing her head to avoid looking into his eyes any longer.

She turned around and walked away, glancing around the room as she began searching for any sign of Helena's presence. Much to her dismay, her necklace warmed the further she got from Erik.

Catherine planned to visit Helena the next day, trying once more to convince the vampire to help her. Exhausted and wounded, Catherine wandered down the hall to get her wounds tended to.

14

Catherine's body ached even more than after Helena unhorsed her at the tournament. She wanted to sleep for days, but the fact that both vampires had infiltrated the manor weighed heavy. She pulled her blankets up to her chin, wrapping herself in soft linens and closing herself off to the world for a few hours.

If vampires didn't kill her first, the sorrow of watching the life she built for herself wither away would.

No matter how she tried to push it out of her mind, the memories of her beloved mentor hissing at her haunted her thoughts. Those glowing red eyes blazed their way through the darkness behind her eyelids. She shook her head to dispel those memories that ghosted through every thought. Though she was sure she'd cried all the tears she had left, her eyes watered once more as she folded her lips between her teeth.

The bruises covering the majority of her body were still quite tender. Catherine scratched her forearms, irritating the skin she'd scrubbed raw when she washed the blood off herself.

She focused on the crackle of the fireplace, breathing in and out slowly to calm her overworking mind. Slowly but surely, she pushed the memories of the undead Walter to the back of her mind.

Part of her longed for the simplicity that came before the tournament. Before impossible tasks, and vampires, and unimaginable grief became the centre of her life.

Something sharp ran across her neck. It stung similarly to Walter's claws when he had grabbed her neck, except this time her skin wasn't broken.

Her heart stopped for a second as she stared into a pair of glowing crimson irises. She went to cry out but a pale hand clamped her mouth to muffle any sound she made.

The woman straddling her stomach softly shushed her. Her fiery red hair fell down her shoulders in waves and her lush pink lips framed a pair of sharp white fangs. The vampire grinned as she playfully ran her other hand down Catherine's side.

Adrenaline surged through Catherine, pulling her out of her fatigued state. She went to sit up, but was pushed back down before she could get her bearings.

'Hush,' Helena scolded, grinning down at the knight with mischievous glee.

There was something in her expression that intrigued Catherine. It was curious, yet still dangerous.

Helena tilted her head to the side as her smile widened.

Catherine tried to speak but her words came out muffled. She frowned and glanced down at Helena's hand.

'You wish to speak?'

Catherine nodded.

'Fine. I'll rip your throat out if you scream.'

'Why are you—'

Helena was quick to cut Catherine off. 'The people were oh so chatty after you dispatched that fledgling. Some of the knights I spoke to were very proud of you. Your technique is quite good, especially since you didn't bother to gird your loins. If I hadn't taken part in the tournament, you may have actually won.'

Once more, Helena had stunned Catherine into silence.

She remained pinned against her mattress, sorting through the tsunami of thoughts that threatened to overwhelm her.

'Thank you?' Catherine finally replied, her voice low and uncertain.

Catherine remembered that Helena had been there, watching the fight in silence. Rage–and strangely, embarrassment–flushed through her system. Warmth spread across her cheeks. She balled her hands into fists and raised an eyebrow at Helena, trying her best to appear only confused instead of the maelstrom of emotions swirling inside her.

'What were you and Erik doing here?' she demanded.

Helena's glee waned at Catherine's question.

'He was here to ensure that Walter reawakened and caused chaos in the manor. I was trailing Erik, hoping to catch him unawares but he let the fledgling out before I could stop him. Chasing a fledgling is harder than herding sheep. Fledglings have no idea what they're capable of yet and they just want blood by any means. He found the crowd of nobles and, well, you know the rest.'

Catherine's eyes were wide. Her eyebrows almost hit

her hairline. She stared up at the vampire in disbelief. 'You knew what was happening and you stood there, doing nothing?'

'Would you rather have three vampires brawl with any nearby humans becoming collateral? Or have you fight the fledgling while my presence keeps Erik from joining him?' Helena asked in reply, glaring down at the knight with annoyance. 'I know you'd find it hard to trust the word of a vampire, but I wouldn't leave you to fight Erik on your own. The last thing the two of us needed was panic and confronting Erik when I didn't have to would've done so.'

The knight let a frustrated breath stream out of her nose. 'You've made your point.'

Helena's expression brightened as she smiled smugly at Catherine. She patted her cheek with her free hand, humming. 'I wouldn't let him kill you. If you were faltering, I would've stepped in,' she said.

'Why?' the knight asked, looking up at the vampire in confusion.

'It's like I said when I first tasted your blood,' Helena said, shaking her head in amusement. She leant over and pressed her nose against Catherine's, staring into the knight's blue irises. 'If you die, I have to go find another human who tastes as good as you do. That could take months, even years. Why should I have to go through that when I found you?'

Catherine tried her best to ignore the smell of copper that wafted from Helena's lips.

'Should I be worried if my father has tried to befriend Erik?'

The grin upon the vampire's lips slowly waned as she let

the knight's words sink in. Crinkles appeared on the bridge of her nose. She ran her tongue over her teeth and glanced at the ceiling before she returned her gaze to the woman underneath her.

'That bastard has been around much longer than I have. As violent as he is, Erik has some decorum. He's likely digging for information about Birkstead and its defences. Pray to your God that he doesn't take an interest in your little village, or that you don't ever cross swords with him.'

Catherine slowly slid her hand underneath her mattress, keeping her upper arm as still as possible whilst she felt around for her dagger.

'You seem like you know him well. Do you?' Catherine asked, narrowing her eyes and watching Helena's reaction.

'The only vampires that don't know what he's like are fledglings, or the ones that don't intermingle with other vampires,' she said, rolling her eyes. 'Vampire politics; it's not something you mortals need to be concerned about.'

The knight grasped the handle of her dagger. She glared right into the vampire's eyes, remaining as still as possible.

'You can't keep using vampire politics as an excuse to avoid my questions,' she said.

The vampire chuckled. She ran the tip of her nail down Catherine's cheek, leaving a tingling trail in her wake.

Catherine did her best to keep her expression stony and hostile.

'You have a point, dear Catherine,' Helena crooned. 'You want to know more about vampires? Who am I to keep you from doing so?'

The knight slid the blade up against the side of her body, keeping the dagger flat against the mattress. She spread her palm over the hilt of the weapon to further camouflage it underneath her blankets. A different type of panic swept through her chest and settled in her belly as Helena's lips playfully brushed her cheek. She couldn't forget Helena was a blood-sucking monster, but that didn't stop her body from yearning for the vampire's touch.

Helena glanced down at Catherine's scabbed neck. 'It's not fair. You smell delicious. If I weren't so in control of my temptations, I would drain you dry just to taste you for more than a few moments.'

Helena forced a breath to roll over Catherine's skin, chilling her healing wounds and making her shiver more violently than she already was. She widened her mouth and went to bite down on Catherine's neck.

Catherine's free hand shot out from underneath the blankets, gripping a handful of Helena's fiery locks. She yanked her head back and pressed the edge of her dagger up against the vampire's throat with her other hand. She clenched her stomach to keep herself sitting up if the vampire tried to push her back down.

'Not so eager to try and drain me with a hunk of silver at your throat, are you?' Catherine teased.

The vampire hissed as her skin either side of the blade reddened and blistered.

'I know you know more than you let on. Tell me what you know about Erik.'

'Persistent, aren't you?' Helena spat.

'I wasn't ordained a knight for only knowing how to use a sword,' Catherine replied, matching Helena's vicious tone. 'Now, tell me what you know about Erik.'

The corner of her lip curled into a nasty smirk as she regarded Catherine with amusement. 'Did you not hear me, or did defeating a fledgling inflate your ego? He's not someone you want to meet on the battlefield.'

Catherine pressed the dagger closer against Helena's neck.

Helena winced.

'He is responsible for the destruction of the village chapel and the creation of a fledgling,' Catherine said. 'Dangerous or not, I cannot allow him to terrorise the people of Birkstead. It is my duty to protect them. I can't protect them from a threat I haven't properly evaluated. Tell me everything.'

Helena drew her hand away from Catherine's throat and sighed.

'You're no fun,' she teased, pouting playfully. When she got no reaction out of Catherine, she dropped the act and frowned in annoyance. 'Fine. He's one of the oldest vampires I know of. Erik does not play well with others. He destroyed the coven he created because the woman he'd reawakened and taken as a lover despised how possessive he was of her. While blood-lust is a trait of vampirism, he embodies that and then some. Most vampires, even the ones he reawakens, give him a wide berth. I confronted him that night in Birkstead about hunting in my territory. You saw how well that went.'

She examined the vampire's expression and had a

feeling she was hiding more. That, however, was not what Catherine immediately focused on.

'Your territory? Since when did you stake your claim on my family's village?'

Catherine kept the dagger at Helena's throat but released her hair. She shifted back against her pillow to support her fatigued body.

'This has been part of my territory for a little while now. I've been on the cusp of your village for a decade, living off a rather wholesome diet of the thugs and ruffians who decided to pay the villages and small towns of Northern England a visit when the moon sits high in the sky,' Helena replied. 'I drew little attention to myself. At least until Erik showed back up. I hope he doesn't scare away my usual prey; I'd have to look elsewhere in the village for food and you'd despise me even more for that, wouldn't you?'

'If you so much as think about hurting anyone in Birkstead, I will cut your pretty little head off, mount it above my fireplace and wear the rest of your ashes around my neck to ensure that you cannot harm anyone again,' Catherine warned.

'You think I'm pretty?' Helena teasingly asked. Her cadence was almost musical.

Helena flinched when Catherine pushed the silver against her flesh.

A blood-lusting smirk touched Helena's lips as she felt Catherine's blood pulse furiously against her inner thighs. Even as her throat burned against the edge of the knight's blade, she couldn't help but to find Catherine's rage adorable. Helena straightened up, moving away from the dagger whilst keeping her weight on Catherine's stomach.

'You really do think I'm pretty, don't you?' the vampire questioned, wiggling her eyebrows at her.

'Stop it!'

Catherine's brows furrowed. Her face heated, colouring her cheeks and forehead red. She gritted her teeth and bared them at the vampire still on top of her. The arches of her feet flexed to the point of pain. Her fingers cramped as she clenched her hands tighter. Her breaths shallowed as she glared up at Helena. Tears of anger and sorrow welled in her eyes as her constantly conflicting thoughts began to overwhelm her. The knight's arms trembled ever so slightly. She swung her blade at Helena, missing when the vampire ducked out of her reach.

'Such anger from someone who is supposed to embody valour. I wonder what your father would say? No... I wonder what Walter would say if he saw you threaten to behead someone you held at knifepoint?' Helena asked.

The vampire jumped off Catherine's hips and draped herself across the nearest windowsill faster than Catherine could blink. Helena pressed her hand up against her throat, frowning when she felt the pustules bordering her new wound. The veins in that area turned grey and would stay that way until she next fed.

With Helena's weight off her body, the knight sat up properly. She held the dagger out towards the vampire. Her breaths mimicked her heartbeat; fast and hard without allowance for rationality or logic.

'Don't you dare say his name! He didn't deserve to be made a monster. He didn't deserve to be slain twice before he

140

could rest. His fate was one worthy of a villain, not someone like him.'

Blood trickled down Helena's pale skin and over the hand she held against her wound. Helena pushed her hair away from her neck with her other hand and sighed.

'I hope you realise that truly valiant knights are the rarest of your kind. Most use their power to further their own goals and fulfil the wants they masquerade as needs. They will use you and discard you when you have nothing left to give them. If he truly was as noble as you say, you were lucky to have him as a mentor,' Helena said. Her face relaxed, revealing the hurt and sorrow she usually kept behind near impenetrable barriers. Before Catherine could protest, she continued to speak. 'The knights I met before you have been philandering brigands who valued money and status over anything else. I know what brigands are like, and a lot of knights tend to be worse.'

'It sounds like someone had their heart broken and is still bitter about it,' Catherine remarked, her tone as sharp as her dagger.

Helena's back straightened. 'What does it matter to you?'

The knight looked down at the blade in her hand, watching how the firelight danced upon the silver. Spots of Helena's blood balanced upon the edge, threatening to fall upon her linens.

Catherine glanced up at the vampire, raising an eyebrow at her. Her thoughts danced with empathy and curiosity regarding Helena's distaste for knights. She kept her jaw taut and her fists clenched, reminding herself that the vampire could very well use her words to catch her off guard again.

141

'I wish to know what traits to avoid acquiring,' Catherine answered. 'Just because my peers do not value their responsibilities doesn't mean that I will end up the same.'

'Given your obsession with Walter's goodness and protecting people who don't even know you, that's not something you need to worry about.' Her playful smile returned to her lips as she noticed that she'd hit a nerve in the same way that Catherine had done just before. 'In seriousness, I don't believe you have the heart to commit even half of the atrocities I've witnessed over the years.'

Catherine kept the tip of her dagger pointed at Helena. Her expression softened as she watched the haunted glaze that shrouded the vampire's eyes. 'You say that, yet I couldn't imagine spending decades as a blood-thirsty creature,' Catherine commented. She narrowed her eyes at the vampire. 'How do you live with yourself, knowing what you and your kind are capable of? How do you see yourself as better than brigands and even the most corrupt knights when you feed off defenceless humans?'

The vampire's red dress fluttered around her calves as she jumped off the windowsill with the grace of a house cat. She stalked over to the door and opened it with ease. Helena turned to Catherine, smiling wide enough to put her fangs on full display.

'It's not so bad being a vampire. Women like you and I benefit from it greatly. It gives you freedom and power. You could have it all and not have to marry someone to have what you want,' Helena explained. 'And vampires don't need to solely live off human blood. Animal blood can satiate us just as well. You don't need to drain something dry in order to survive, some people are willing to part with some blood if you offer payment in return. There are humane ways to ensure you stay well-fed.'

A Knight's Blood

Catherine remained silent. The point of her dagger remained trained on Helena.

The vampire sighed at the knight's refusal to speak. She shrugged as her smile fell from her face.

'Suit yourself. You might come around to the idea,' Helena replied. She went to take a step out into the hall before turning back to the knight. 'Oh, and Catherine? You'll need more than fancy footwork, luck, and silver to kill me.'

Before Catherine could even blink, Helena disappeared. A breeze floated through the air from where she had just been.

After a few moments of silence, Catherine got out of bed, closed the door, and snuggled back underneath the blankets again. She held her dagger close to her chest and kept her eyes on the door. Her eyelids became way too heavy to keep open. Unable to let her adrenaline overpower her fatigue, she finally succumbed to sleep's irresistible allure.

15

Though the day had barely begun, a fog descended over Catherine the moment she woke up. The constant fatigue and battle of thoughts and emotions weighed heavy upon her. Sorrow, worry, and grief took its toll on her, draining most of her energy and leaving her numb.

She missed Walter. She longed for the chance to ask him for advice one more time. Memories of his unfaltering belief in her brought tears to her eyes for the first time of what would be many during the day.

It was the day of her mentor's funeral, after all. She had to remain as composed as possible, even if all she wanted to do was scream and cry the entire time.

Catherine started her day as if nothing was wrong, preparing to pretend like she wasn't trapped in a nightmare she couldn't wake up from.

The scent of wildflowers drifted through the morning breeze as Catherine went down to Birkstead with various tarts, pies, and treats, as well as some mead and wine, to treat the people without her father knowing. The kitchen staff, however, were aware of her plans ahead of time and were more than happy to help.

The way the villagers' faces lit up when they saw the food and drink Catherine brought down to them broke through the cloud that hung over her. It didn't dispel it completely, but the break from her grief was welcomed. The foreman informed her that they'd had no further issues regarding mercenaries that night. That news pleased her more than she could voice.

Thankfully, her father kept his word. A pair of knights strode through Birkstead upon their horses, the three nodding to each other in acknowledgement.

She checked on the young woman from yesterday, relieved to see that she was feeling better. Catherine spent some time with the girl and her friends, teaching them self-defence tips with the brooches on their clothes. She smiled as the girls laughed at their own missteps and wobbly stances, wishing that she could return to a time where she could act the same during her training.

She stayed in Birkstead for a few hours before she had to return to the manor in time for Walter's funeral, though there was nothing left physically to bless. His remains were already on their way to the Holy See.

The funeral itself was a blur. Catherine remembered the sympathetic hugs she received from Aldric and Sabina, but everything else refused cement themselves in her mind. She heard what the priest had to say, but it didn't properly register. Memories of Walter continued to replay whilst she stared at the altar, her eyes glazing over.

The mental fog finally began to lift as the funeral concluded and they were dismissed by the priest.

Geoffrey stood in front of the altar and insisted that the knights and nobles present adjourn to the Great Hall for the refreshments he had organised.

Catherine slipped away from the crowd and hid amongst

145

the shadows, waiting for the distance between her and them to lengthen. The moment she felt they were far enough, she turned towards the manor chapel and crept back towards it. Her steps were as quiet as she could make them. She rounded the corner and went the long way back to the chapel so she didn't run into anyone.

A quick glance over her shoulder confirmed that no one initially noticed her leave. They, especially Geoffrey and Aldric, would eventually notice that she wasn't there, but that wasn't something she worried about.

The soft voices of fellow mourners and the raucous laughter of conversing lords followed her down the corridor, bouncing along the stone as if they were whispers from the spirits of past nobles voicing their disappointment in her.

Upon reaching the chapel, she opened the door and slipped into the empty room, closing it behind her. She slid the bolt into place and leant against the door, smacking her back against the wood.

Catherine's chest tightened as tears finally fell from her lashes. She did her best to muffle her sobs to avoid being discovered. She reached up and grasped the cross, pulling on the pendant so that the chain dug into the back of her neck. She'd never experienced the sensation of drowning, but felt as if this was as close as she was going to get. She stood in almost complete darkness, away from everyone. Finally, she had the chance to let herself openly feel her pain.

Or so she thought.

'Looks like someone's not handling the pressure well,' a familiar voice teased.

Catherine lifted her head up and looked down the aisle

towards the altar, spying a pair of softly glowing red irises. Her hand went straight to the dagger on her belt.

The sunlight that streamed into the chapel during the funeral was no longer there. She glanced at the stained-glass windows: heavy red curtains had been pulled over them to keep the sun's yellowed light from entering the room.

A hum of amusement echoed.

Catherine's heart beat hard and fast against her ribs as she watched the outline of the vampire get closer, Helena's crimson eyes boring into her own glassy blue ones. Shivers ran down her spine. Heat travelled through her body and settled in her stomach. She slid the dagger from its sheath and held it firmly in front of her.

Helena stared at her with a mischievous smirk that was barely visible in the shadows.

'What's the matter, vampire got your tongue?' Helena purred.

'Why do you care?' Catherine snapped. 'It's not like monsters have feelings.'

Helena narrowed her eyes at Catherine and grabbed either side of the knight's chin, squeezing her cheeks. 'My heart doesn't beat anymore but it can still feel pain.'

'What do you want, Helena?' Catherine asked, her voice wavering from the copious amount of mucus coating her throat.

The knight clenched her teeth, trying her best not to wince as the ache in her jaw returned. Her tears trickled down her cheeks and caressed Helena's fingertips. She tilted the dagger's tip up towards the vampire's throat in warning, which had fully healed since the night before.

Helena's hand drifted down from Catherine's chin and wrapped loosely around her throat. She brought her lips close to Catherine's face and tilted the knight's head, looking down intensely at her sorrow-filled eyes and tear-streaked cheeks. The vampire softly clicked her tongue, keeping her tone light and playful.

'Can't I say hello to my favourite knight in her time of need?'

Helena's tongue licked the tip of Catherine's nose before she leant back and chuckled at the confusion blooming upon the knight's face. The quick, erratic beating of Catherine's heart excited Helena. The sensation of hearing and feeling it made her giddy.

Catherine remained silent, sniffing back the tears that continued to slicken her cheeks.

The vampire released Catherine's throat before she disappeared, reappearing behind the altar a moment later. Helena cleared the altar of anything that didn't serve her. She picked up a tinderbox and lit the candle she left on top of the black altar cloth.

The light from the flame danced upon the vampire's face, illuminating her as she closed her eyes and held her hands out over the candle. Helena's prayer to the Morrígan flowed from her tongue as if every word she whispered was wine. Even if Catherine couldn't understand her, she spoke her mother tongue of Middle Gaelic effortlessly as she pleaded with the goddess to watch over the fallen knight.

After a few seconds of tense silence, Helena moved her

hand away from the flame and opened her eyes. The vampire returned her crimson gaze to Catherine once more, tilting her head a little as she watched the knight from across the room.

'I came to see if Erik has heard a whisper of your idea to kill him yet,' Helena replied. 'Or if he'd done anything else you were aware of.'

The ghost of Helena's touch lingered upon Catherine's neck. She held the dagger down by her side as she walked down the aisle towards the altar.

The vampire lounged against the altar without a single care for how she appeared. She played with the fabric that pooled around her legs, waving the skirts back and forth as if she were manipulating streams of blood.

The candle flickered as the vampire sprung up onto the altar and sat on the front edge, crossing one leg over the other. Helena leant back on the heel of her palm and cocked her head to the side, sweeping her stray hairs away from her eyes with her other hand.

'Nothing in regards to him has come up. At least not yet,' Catherine announced. 'And you should not be sitting on an altar like that. It's blasphemous.'

'When you live for more than a few decades, you realise this isn't as damning as you're made to believe,' Helena replied. 'It's simply one of the many ways in which society attempts to keep you in your place. I wasn't jesting with you when I said that reawakening was the best thing to happen to me. How else will you gain the independence you desire and the power you need to protect the people?'

The knight drew in a sharp breath and straightened her

shoulders. Her nose crinkled with abhorrence at Helena's words and her own curious thoughts about them. She pursed her lips and stomped forward, pointing the dagger at Helena.

'You found out your answer, now leave,' Catherine commanded.

Helena's smirk widened into a predatory grin. She was sitting on the altar in one second and on top of Catherine in the next. The speed and strength the vampire possessed always caught the knight by surprise.

Catherine yelped as she was knocked to the floor and pinned to the red runner underneath her. Her head slammed against the carpet and the stone underneath it.

Helena wrapped her hands around Catherine's wrists, pinning her to the floor. The vampire pressed her body against the knight underneath her. She couldn't help but to revel in how fast Catherine's blood rushed through her body.

A scowl settled on the knight's face as she glared up at Helena.

'No, I don't think I will leave,' Helena purred. She ran her tongue over her fangs and grinned down at Catherine. The pupils in her eyes slowly dilated, dimming some of the crimson glow. 'This manor is rather exquisite. It's much better than the ruins I've been hiding in.'

She kept her gaze locked with the vampire's. She tried to keep her breathing and heartbeat steady.

'The only way you'll reside here is if you're nothing more than fangs and ashes,' Catherine spat in response.

Helena pouted and made a soft, saddened sound that

pulled at Catherine's heart-strings. It was playful, but there was something vulnerable about it.

The vampire's smirk returned moments later.

'Oh, that's unfortunate,' Helena replied. 'Then what will you do when another vampire shows up? You won't be able to kill someone like Erik by yourself, vampire slayer.'

Catherine opened her mouth to respond, but the words died upon her tongue. She sighed and pressed her lips together, choosing to remain silent instead of further fuelling Helena's teasing.

Helena had a point, but Catherine didn't want to admit it. Even if she had Aldric's help, she wouldn't even know how to weed Erik out of her father's circle now that he had inserted himself into it. Whether she liked it or not, Helena's affinity for interacting with nobles proved useful if frustrating.

Catherine turned her head to avoid Helena's gaze.

'That's what I thought,' Helena replied, her voice no louder than a whisper.

'Whether I die or not, I will do whatever it takes to protect the people and ensure some control over my life,' Catherine proclaimed. 'If I have to challenge Erik in the middle of a social event, then that's what I have to do.'

Helena rolled her eyes. 'And I thought vampires were dramatic.'

'You think you're so funny, don't you?' Catherine remarked with a raised eyebrow.

'I like to think so. Vampires lose a lot of things when

Gwendolyn K. Blackthorne

they reawaken, but they very rarely lose their sense of humour,'
Helena said. 'Vampires tend to gain more from undeath than we
lost from our mortal lives.'

'There is nothing you can say that will make me want to
become a monster like you,' Catherine snapped in reply.

'Is that so?' Helena said, lowering her voice. 'I can be
rather compelling when the situation calls for it.'

Catherine's expression betrayed almost nothing, even as
curiosity surged through her mind.

Tension slithered through the air amongst the smoke that
twisted into the air above them. The remnants of the frankin-
cense and myrrh burned during the mass danced through the air
alongside the smoke, the heady and rich scents clouding Catherine's head.

Catherine only heard silence. Her world span around her,
centring on the only stable thing in her vision, Helena.

Helena focused on the sweet symphony that was Catherine's breaths, heartbeat, and the quiet crackling of candle flames.
Helena took the knight's prolonged silence as a challenge.

Not wanting to prolong the silence between them any
longer, she closed her eyes and brought her lips to Catherine's.

Panic clutched Catherine's chest. Her breath didn't reach
her lungs.

The idea of kissing a vampire didn't disgust her—in
fact, it excited her. She'd never been kissed before. She had
resigned herself to the thought that she'd eventually be kissed,
but wouldn't be able to enjoy the experience. In that moment,
Catherine decided that maybe she could like being kissed. At

least, she was willing to try it.

The knight closed her eyes and stayed still, allowing Helena to kiss her.

Helena's lips touched hers.

Because the rest of her actions towards Catherine so far had been rough, it surprised her that the vampire was so gentle with her now. Catherine refused to move, even to take a breath or swallow her saliva. This tender moment was as close to bliss as she'd ever experienced.

That one kiss confirmed to Catherine that the vampire's lips were indeed as soft as she thought they would be. Helena's fangs didn't get in the way if Helena didn't want them to, and Catherine wondered for a moment if she wanted them to.

A frantic knock sounded at the door, breaking the silence that enveloped the two women.

Helena drew back, looking up at the door. Her crimson eyes were wide and her fangs bared in case that sound indicated an oncoming threat.

'Cat?'

Catherine's eyes widened as she recognised the voice calling for her.

Aldric.

'Hide,' Catherine ordered with a harsh whisper.

Helena nodded and dashed behind the altar, slipping into the priest's chambers behind the tabernacle. The door closed behind her.

The chapel was left in almost complete darkness once more. Whatever light came into the room was let in through the cracks of the chapel door and the candle Helena had lit before.

Catherine slipped her dagger back into its sheath and let out a short breath to steady her beating heart in case it betrayed her.

He knocked again. 'Cat? Are you in there?'

She hurried towards the chapel door, smoothing her hair and dress as she went.

The bolt whined as she slid it back and opened the door.

Aldric stood on the other side in a black tunic, his sword hanging from his belt. His face was red and blotchy around his glassy eyes. He greeted her with a sad, tired smile.

'You weren't in the Great Hall,' Aldric remarked, although it sounded more like a question.

'I don't wish for anyone to see me cry,' Catherine replied. 'Least of all my father. I don't want to give him anything else to use against me.'

Aldric brushed a few stray hairs away from Catherine's forehead.

'Catherine, you can't keep running away from your father. The only way to show him that you're fit to lead is to challenge him and prove him wrong,' he said.

Catherine tried her best not to nod in agreement while the older knight fussed over her hair in the same way she'd seen his wife do so with their daughter.

'You're right,' she replied. 'I need to prove that I'm more

than just some thing to be married off. Even if that fledgling was Walter, I've killed a vampire. I doubt many knights here in Birkstead can boast that. And if I can kill a vampire, I can prove myself as a leader.'

The older knight smiled a bit wider and gave Catherine a playful pat on her shoulder.

'That's what I want to hear.' Aldric's smile faltered as he sighed. 'Speaking of vampires, have you made any progress?'

She glanced over at Aldric, noticing that the older knight was looking anywhere but at her. While odd, she understood.

Grief caused even the most predictable person to become unpredictable.

'Yes, but it's more dire than I first thought,' Catherine replied. 'Unfortunately, two vampires have infiltrated Birkstead's social sphere. So, that complicates things.'

Aldric stopped mid-step and looked at Catherine with widened eyes. His posture stiffened as he watched her continue down the hall. He began to follow, keeping a step or two behind her so he could keep an eye on her body language.

'Truly?' he asked.

She nodded. 'One is aware I know about her. I'm hoping the second hasn't caught on yet. He's meant to be the more dangerous one of the two. I'm at a loss for how to proceed and would appreciate your advice on the matter.'

He remained silent for a few moments. His eyes darted around the hallway as he gathered his thoughts.

Catherine stopped walking and turned to look over her

shoulder at Aldric.

The older knight realised that she was waiting for an answer and hurried to her side. Aldric cleared his throat and nodded. 'Of course. We should discuss it later, when there is less risk of other nobles hearing. The last thing we need is panic arising due to this information spreading further.'

'Agreed,' Catherine said. 'Thank you.'

'You're welcome. Come now, let's show them how competent you are,' Aldric said, laying an arm around her shoulder and leading her down the hall.

She peered over her shoulder to see a pair of crimson eyes in the darkness, watching her.

16

A wall of voices hit Catherine as she entered the Great Hall. The loudest snippets of gossip and laughter made her blood boil. She clenched her fists and resisted the urge to clench her jaw as well. Catherine moved her hand away from her dagger, reminding herself that it was there as a decoration of rank.

'I know you hate this, but you have to make an appearance. It's your duty,' Aldric chastised. 'Sabina would be more than happy to walk the room with you if wish to appear as if you're interacting without participating much.'

Catherine pursed her lips and sighed.

Aldric was right.

She pushed her worries aside and forced a convincing smile onto her lips. Catherine tilted her chin up and walked into the room, Aldric following close behind.

Aldric made his way to the table in the centre of the room and helped himself to some fig pastries. He smiled at two approaching knights and dove into conversation with them, leaving Catherine to navigate the social battlefield by herself.

The stone room had been decorated with varying black fabrics, soaking in the light emitting from crackling braziers.

Funeral or not, her father spared no expense.

Servants made their way around the room with trays of

wine, mead, and food for those who hadn't made their way towards the table adorned with various carefully prepared dishes. The beautiful scents of freshly baked bread, spiced meat, and fruit filled pastries filled the air.

Delicious food and strong drink seemed to lift the spirits of the people in the Great Hall. Though most were dressed in various items of black and grey clothing, they grouped together in their usual cliques as if they were attending one of her father's usual events.

Loud jumbled conversations peppered with fits of chuckles echoed around the room, clashing with the thoughts that ran through Catherine's head.

Catherine closed her eyes and let out a breath to better steady herself. No matter how she tried to banish her panic from her mind, she couldn't. She knew what panic was, but ever since she met Helena, it took on a new form that gripped both her heart and soul. All she could do was freeze when the vampire gave her a fanged grin. The panic and yearning hit her harder than falling from Smokey did. Just thinking about the fact that the copper-haired beauty stole her first kiss made her insides melt. Catherine almost wished that Aldric hadn't banged on the chapel door.

She winced, shaking her head whilst mentally chastising herself for her thoughts. Not only was she daydreaming about kissing someone, but she was daydreaming about kissing a vampire. Knights were supposed to kill vampires, not pine after them.

A servant bowed to Catherine and offered her a tankard of mead, pulling her from her ruminations. Catherine took the tankard with a small nod.

Catherine cradled the tankard in her hand and held it

close to her stomach, looking around the room to see what her conversation prospects were.

Her lord father amicably talked with a man in fine green clothes adorned with gold and jewels.

Said man's braided golden hair was all she needed to recognise him. Erik.

It only took her a moment to decide that she would avoid those two for as long as she could. The longer she could have him believe she didn't know he was a vampire, the better.

The mead danced upon her tongue as she took a small sip. It was strong and smooth, just how she liked it.

Catherine looked around for Aldric and found him speaking with the same two other knights from before and his wife, Sabina.

Sabina held herself with the decorum and grace Catherine could never achieve, even if she was tutored day and night to do so. Sabina stood next to her husband with her head high, a beautiful smile upon her face, and a goblet in her hand. The woman was absolutely radiant. She grasped her husband's forearm and stood by his side, staring lovingly at him as he regaled his comrades with an anecdote about teaching one of the new squires how to ride a horse.

The two other knights beamed as Aldric spoke, his hands going everywhere as he acted out what he was saying. The laughter they shared was infectious and brought a small smile to Catherine's lips even from across the room.

Catherine thought back to Aldric's suggestion of walking the room with Sabina and heavily considered that option, swirling her mead around in her tankard as she did so.

With her mind made up, she wandered over to Aldric, Sabina, and the two other knights, forcing a smile onto her face to appear as friendly as she could muster. Much to Catherine's relief, Sabina was the first to turn and acknowledge her. Sabina's gentle smile helped soothe the chaos that ravaged her mind.

'Lady Seymour, I'm so glad you're here,' Sabina said, giving Catherine a small reverent nod. 'Sir Alwyn will be sorely missed by Aldric and I, as I know he will be missed by you as well.'

'Thank you for your kind words,' Catherine replied, returning the nod. 'He was loved by all and memories of him will be well cherished. I'm feeling peckish and the food looks delightful. Would you care to join me?'

'Of course. I've been wanting to see what the kitchen staff have come up with. Have fun, my love,' Sabina said, pressing a kiss to Aldric's cheek before leaving his side.

She linked arms with the lady knight and sipped some of the wine from the goblet in her hand. Sabina glanced at Catherine and gave her a small nudge.

'Lead the way, my lady,' Sabina said.

The two women strolled around the edge of the room, avoiding getting too close to the clusters of nobles that stared at them.

Catherine's shoulders dropped after spending only a few moments in Sabina's presence. She couldn't explain why, but there was something about her soft demeanour that served to calm her no matter what the situation was. Like Aldric, Sabina was one of the only people in her father's court she felt she could trust wholeheartedly.

'I don't know how many people have told you this, but I'm sure that Walter would be just as proud of you as Aldric and I are,' Sabina said, breaking the silence between them. Her voice was gentle and low, louder than a whisper but quiet enough to blend into the noise around them. 'But that doesn't help ease any of your guilt and grief, does it?'

'It doesn't. In fact, it only made it worse,' Catherine replied.

'Why?'

'If I had beheaded him back in Birkstead, no one would've gotten hurt and he wouldn't have been killed for a second time. My sentimentality made everything so much harder than it needed to be.'

'Cat,' Sabina said. 'You can't blame yourself. Only the most hardened of hearts would be able to do that, and I'm sure it would still affect them afterwards. Be gentle with yourself, you don't have to be made of steel all the time.'

'I'm meant to protect people from harm. I didn't do what was required of me and people suffered because of it.'

Sabina sighed and looked at Catherine out of corner of her eyes. 'People make mistakes. No matter who you are or how careful you are, you're bound to make an unwise decision more than once in your life. It's how we learn and grow. I'm sure that if the roles were reversed, Walter couldn't go through with beheading you.'

'Thanks,' Catherine replied.

A smile tugged at the edges of Catherine's lips for a few

moments before it fell.

'You're welcome,' Sabina said, sipping some more of her wine before she began speaking again. 'I'm not a knight, so I don't know firsthand what it's like to have someone's safety in their hands. But I do know a few things that apply across multiple lifestyles. Now, how about we see if they made fresh tarts?'

'Absolutely,' Catherine replied, squeezing Sabina's arm with her own.

The two women walked towards the table of food, exchanging pleasantries when necessary. Sabina took Catherine's almost empty tankard from her and handed both it and her goblet to a passing servant, freeing their hands to pick the treats that caught their fancies.

The moment Catherine spotted the plate of custard tarts, she immediately grabbed one, taking a bite too big to be considered ladylike. She hummed with delight, relishing in how the eggy pastry felt upon her tongue.

Sabina chuckled at Catherine's childlike adoration and went for a piece of pale rosewater nougat. She daintily nibbled the end and surveyed the room for her husband, accidentally meeting Lord Seymour's gaze instead.

Geoffrey spied his daughter beside Aldric's wife and pointed at her, waving her over.

A frown fell upon her kind face as she turned to Catherine, catching her stuffing the rest of her custard tart into her mouth. Despite knowing she was the bearer of bad news, Sabina laughed at Catherine's adorable tart-stuffed cheeks.

'Your father wishes to speak with you,' Sabina said and pointed her father out as he beckoned for his daughter once more.

'Very well,' Catherine sighed. 'Let's pray he's not going to start an argument.'

'You'll be alright,' Sabina replied, patting her shoulder.

Catherine sighed again and made her way over to where her father stood with Erik.

Her expression changed as she saw a familiar head of red hair make her way through the crowd, finding someone to strike up a conversation with.

Helena looked as though if nothing had happened earlier in the chapel: no blood, no burns, no patches of grey flesh. Nothing. She exuded the same ethereal beauty she always seemed in command of. She wasn't wearing the tattered dress she'd worn in the chapel, instead she wore a pristine gown as green as the leaves of a juniper tree. Leaves and flowers were embroidered in a delicate pale green along her sleeves and hemline. The dress made Helena's hair shine like polished copper near a flame.

Catherine clenched her teeth and tore her gaze away from the vampire that kissed her.

Geoffrey smiled widely when Catherine joined his side.

'Ah, there's my Catherine. My only daughter. The light of my life,' he announced, his words slurring slightly.

She raised an eyebrow at her father's words. Other times he'd been drunk, he'd never been this nice to her. What changed? What game was her father playing?

'Good day, my lord,' Catherine replied.

Laughter tumbled from her father's lips as he patted her on the shoulder a little too hard. His face was flushed red and his breath stank of garlic and wine.

It took all the willpower she had to keep her mouth closed and her attention focused on anything but Erik's blazing crimson irises.

'Isn't she a treasure?' he asked Erik.

She ignored her father and turned to Erik.

He was a tall blond man with stubble along his square jaw. His physique reminded her of a tree trunk. His hands and his neck were adorned with gold jewellery unlike anything she'd ever seen. The emeralds and rubies were dull but impressive. The way Erik carried himself was indictive that he was a warrior, even if he didn't carry a weapon at the moment.

The blond stared at Catherine, refusing to lift his gaze from the knight's uncomfortable expression. He gave her a lop-sided smile that exposed one of his fangs.

'A treasure indeed,' he said, his Danish accent thick and heavy.

Catherine bit her tongue. She narrowed her eyes at him and forced a smile to her lips, playing nice. She had to continue the charade of being oblivious to what he really was.

'A pleasure to see you again,' Catherine replied and gave him a small nod. 'I hope you've found your time in England and in my father's court hospitable,' she said.

'The food is nowhere near as good as it is in Denmark, but the people are much more agreeable. I'm hoping to put down roots here eventually; it is such a lovely place,' Erik replied.

A Knight's Blood

Geoffrey's chest swelled with drunken pride.

Catherine glanced at her father with unease.

'Birkstead may be one of the smallest villages in the northern provinces, but we produce the finest wool in the country. Even the king himself requests our wool,' Geoffrey said, beaming wide.

'It is quite a quaint little place. I hope to call England home soon,' Erik said.

The way in which the vampire spoke about finding a place for himself sent shivers down Catherine's spine.

She kept her feet planted on the floor and her expression friendly despite wanting to warn her fellow knights of the monsters in their midst. This situation had to be handled with care, or the two vampires could slaughter everyone in the room before anyone could try to defend themselves.

On the other hand, her father had given her a week to track down the vampires behind the destruction of the chapel before he married her off. Given how quickly that deadline was sneaking up on her, she had a bad feeling about where this was going.

'Your wife is a lucky woman,' Catherine said, probing to see if her gut feeling was correct.

'He doesn't have a wife, Catherine. It's one of the reasons why he's here. Danish women apparently aren't up to standard, isn't that right, Erik?' Geoffrey asked, nudging the man with his elbow.

Catherine's stomach dropped.

Erik snorted at her father's joke.

'English women have a certain… something I haven't been able to find anywhere else,' Erik replied.

'Well, I wish you luck on your quest to find a suitable bride,' Catherine said.

Unease spread through her mind like a brewing storm wanting to destroy anything in its path. She had to distract herself before she made an irrational decision and painted a larger target on her back.

She let her gaze wander over the crowd, but Aldric and Sabina were nowhere to be seen.

She did, however, find Helena once more. She caught the vampire watching her. Something in her gaze made Catherine feel strangely comforted.

Their gazes connected for a few seconds before Catherine ever so slightly jerked her head towards Erik.

She turned back to her father and Erik, reminding herself to keep calm.

'I'm sure he will,' Geoffrey said, sounding as though he knew the outcome.

Erik turned to look at Catherine and let his gaze roam her from head to toe.

'Your father says you're unwed. I did not realise that such a beautiful woman doesn't have someone chasing after her.' He shared a conspiring smile with her father.

'I have found that having a husband would hold me back from properly protecting the people of Birkstead. While I am a noblewoman, I am also a knight,' Catherine said, letting her revulsion for that sentiment flow from her tongue eloquently yet venomously. 'We can't produce England's best wool without the shepherds protecting their flocks, the traders selling the wool, the weavers spinning the wool into clothes, rugs, and blankets, or the farmers harvesting crops that feed the entire village. Birkstead needs someone to look out for its residents, not someone that just furthers their own bloodline and lines their pockets with money.'

Geoffrey's expression darkened as he glared at Catherine.

'I apologise for my daughter, Erik. She's strong-willed and often forgets her duties as a noblewoman.' Geoffrey side-eyed his daughter, taking another deep drink from his goblet.

'Having a strong will isn't always a bad thing.' Erik said, a wistful glint in his crimson eyes. 'It can be rather endearing.'

Geoffrey's expression shifted to one of joy and hope. He swished the remnants of his drink around in his goblet and hummed in thought, the cogs in his drunken mind clunking along slowly.

'Is that so?' Geoffrey asked.

'Indeed. What's the point in a boring marriage? There's nothing worse than a life populated by dull people.'

A wonky smile stretched across Geoffrey's face as he pieced together what Erik was insinuating. 'I do have some other suitors in mind for my daughter, but you're welcome to convince me that you're a better option for her.'

Catherine's fingers tightened into fists.

Panic spurred her heart to beat faster and her thoughts

to spiral further.

She had to get out of the Great Hall.

'It was lovely to see you again, Erik, but I'm afraid I must go mingle with some of the other guests. A host's work is never done, I hope you understand,' Catherine said.

The vampire smiled at her and bowed slightly. 'But of course, my lady. I hope to see you again soon.'

She tried to keep her pace steady as she walked away, but she desperately combed the sea of faces for Erik's nemesis.

Her efforts were in vain. She couldn't see her at all.

But she could see Aldric.

She made her way through the crowd towards where Aldric was engaging in conversation with a small group of people. Catherine wove through the drunken nobles and knights, finally reaching him and spotting one of the people listening to him speak.

Helena.

She stopped in front of Aldric and glared at the red-haired vampire.

Helena's fanged smile fell as she noticed the tension on Catherine's face. 'What happened?'

'It seems as if my father is considering marrying me your friend from Denmark,' Catherine replied.

'I'm surprised he showed his face,' Helena muttered.

'You two know each other?' Aldric asked, looking from

Catherine to Helena with surprise.

'Come with me, I'll explain,' Catherine replied.

Catherine began to lead the older knight through the crowded hall. She looked over her shoulder to see that the vampire was following along.

She turned sharply, pointing a finger at Helena. 'You, stay.'

Before Helena could say anything, Catherine grabbed Aldric's hand and practically dragged him out of the Great Hall.

Helena crossed her arms over her chest and pouted.

'Why can't she come with us?' Aldric asked as he followed Catherine out of the hall.

'She's part of the problem.'

The moment they turned the corner, Helena followed.

17

Catherine ushered Aldric into her bedroom and closed the door behind her. She breathed out a sigh of relief and pressed her back against the door. She grasped her cold necklace and took a moment to steady her racing heart. Though it worked in the past, it did nothing to calm her thoughts now. Her mind still whirled faster than any winds she'd ever been caught in. Concern and panic slithered through her thoughts as the cross refused to warm in her palm.

'Can you please tell me why we had to leave so abruptly?' Aldric asked, his expression a mix of confusion and impatience. 'Because I was having a wonderful con-'

'I found the vampires who destroyed the chapel,' Catherine said, cutting him off.

He stared at Catherine in shock. 'What?'

Catherine stepped away from the door. She clutched the cross around her neck with all her might, trying to stop her arms from shaking.

Though Aldric was forbidden to physically help her, lest he forfeit Geoffrey's payments for his daughter's education, he was at least able to give her advice on the situation.

And she desperately needed his advice.

'They're in the Great Hall, pretending to be nobles

A Knight's Blood

mourning the man one of them killed,' Catherine replied.

Aldric grasped the hilt of his blade so tight that he grimaced from how his calloused skin strained to cover his knuckles. The way in which he pursed his lips and glanced at the ground made him seem as if he was hiding something.

'There are two vampires are in the Great Hall right now,' he repeated. 'And we're in your bedroom talking about it?'

Catherine nodded. 'Apart from the vampires themselves, we're the only ones that know.'

Aldric began to pace the room. His hands played with his stubble, covering his mouth with a sigh. Worry creased his forehead deeper than age ever could.

'From what I've learned, they're both accomplished warriors. It'd be unwise for me to confront them without a plan,' she explained in reply. 'Every time I get close enough, there's something that stops me from taking advantage of the situation, namely the crowds of people father invited.'

The older knight did not stop moving. He continued to play with his face nervously, avoiding Catherine's gaze and refusing to say anything about the information she revealed to him.

'I found out which one killed Walter,' Catherine said.

'It wasn't me,' a feminine voice added.

Both knights spun around and stared at the woman standing in the doorway.

'I told you not to follow us,' Catherine said through gritted teeth.

The vampire flashed her fangs in an open smile. She

pranced over to the bed and sat down, cooing as she felt how soft Catherine's bedding was.

'We've known each other for only a short while, but you should know by now that I do what I want,' Helena replied as she crossed one leg over the other and leant back, placing her hands behind her for support. She looked over at Aldric, a smirk touching her lips. 'Unless I'm being paid to do otherwise.'

Catherine blinked, confused as to what Helena was insinuating. She glanced between the two of them, pointing from one to the other with furrowed brows.

'What are you talking about?' she asked as Helena's words were swept away by the chaos already racing through her thoughts.

Helena's laugh echoed around Catherine's bedroom. She looked at Aldric, smiling wider as she realised Catherine didn't hadn't caught onto what she meant. The vampire's tongue touched one of her fangs as she continued to chuckle. 'Should I tell her, or should you?'

'Tell me what?' Catherine demanded. She gritted her teeth as the silver's chill coaxed more goosebumps from her flesh. 'Tell me what, Helena?'

'Your dear Aldric hires me as a mercenary to deal with problems that are too difficult for you mortals. How else do you think I could afford such beautiful garments?' Helena replied, swishing her dark green skirts to make her point.

Catherine could've sworn that her heart stopped. A scoff of disbelief was the only sound she could even think to make. Catherine looked from Aldric to Helena and back again as the re-alisation finally dawned upon her. Hurt and betrayal forced tears to her eyes. Catherine's ribs ached. She turned to Aldric, barely holding back the emotions that grasped her body and refused to let go.

'You knew?' Her words were pained and breathy. 'You knew what she was this entire time and didn't say anything?'

Aldric glanced between Helena and Catherine, holding his breath as he chose his words carefully.

As much as he knew it would hurt her, she needed to know the truth.

'Yes, I knew,' he admitted. 'I've hired her more than once. She's good at tracking down any bounty she gets, even if it's just a predator harassing the villagers' chickens.'

He paused and looked at Helena lounging on Catherine's bed, smiling and smug.

'I also invited her to the tournament.'

'You knew she was the Crusader too?' Catherine questioned, scoffing. 'I can't believe this.'

Catherine blinked a few times. She shook her head as Aldric's words echoed in her mind. Memories of the tournament rushed into the forefront of her mind, remembering how Aldric's squire gladly assisted Helena during her masquerade as the Crusader.

She stared at them, absolutely dumbfounded at how she didn't realise it before.

That was why he was nervous when she spoke to him about vampires. He knew about Helena's presence and didn't bother to say anything before now.

A tear trickled down her face. Catherine swallowed her

saliva and sniffed back the snot that threatened to leak from her nostrils.

'What about your oath to protect the innocent from harm? Doesn't allowing a vampire to live and potentially hurt others go against that?' Catherine asked.

'You tell me,' Aldric replied pointedly. 'Has that oath stopped you from allowing Helena to live, let alone becoming familiar with her?'

Catherine's cheeks turned red. She stared at Aldric, trembling with embarrassment and anger.

No matter how outspoken she claimed to be about the sins and machinations of the Church, she had believed their rhetoric about vampires all the same and assumed other knights felt the same. It wasn't until she met Helena that she even questioned that rhetoric's validity. How many other knights held beliefs that challenged the Church's teachings?

'Why wouldn't you tell me?' Catherine exclaimed, ignoring the hot tears that began streaming down her cheeks.

Aldric sighed. He went to pull her into a hug, hoping it would calm her down enough for him to explain himself.

Catherine dodged his arms, stepping to the side. Her glassy eyes shook as she hugged herself and glared at him with sorrow, anger, and distrust. She distanced herself from Aldric and Helena, walking backwards towards her hearth. Her whole body trembled as her emotions fought for dominance.

The older knight's arms slowly dropped down by his side as he watched Catherine begin to unravel. Aldric knew he had to handle her with care, otherwise the destruction of their relationship was imminent.

'I wanted to protect you,' he replied.

'Don't lie to me!' Catherine jabbed her finger in Aldric's direction, her chest heaving as she struggled to inhale through the building sobs. 'I can protect myself just fine!'

Aldric took a deep breath, keeping himself calm so he didn't feed into the fire that was clearly burning inside Catherine. He forced his body to relax even as he had to remain on high alert.

'I'm not lying,' he explained. 'If you had known about vampires, and Helena's role as an undead mercenary, you would've ended up exactly like your mother. I couldn't let that happen.'

'And what's so wrong with that? She was a wonderful woman who cared about protecting people!'

Aldric wrung his hands, bracing himself for how Catherine was going to react. 'The Church orchestrated her death.'

Catherine's whole body sagged. Everything she knew about her childhood and her mother were shattered. The sorrow that undercut the rest of her emotions took control, squeezing her chest for every little bit of breath that remained.

'What,' was all she could manage in response.

Helena got to her feet and went to reach for Catherine's arm, thinking against it moments later and lowering her hand. The vampire's usual mischievousness was banished from her expression as she recognised the emotions that swirled in Catherine's head. She lowered her crimson eyes towards the floor, unsure of how to help.

'I know you're aware of her time as a researcher for

the Church. But, do you know why they had killed her?' he asked, his expression softening.

Catherine shook her head, unable to voice a response. Tears slickened her cheeks.

'She was a wonderful woman, your mother. The more she researched and the more she got to know some vampires personally, she began to realise that the Church loves to deal in in absolutes. Not all vampires live for the kill, just like not all Christians are compassionate. She tried to make them understand that there were vampires who wanted to protect people from the vampires who meant to do harm. The Church never understood her plight, so they killed her,' Aldric explained. 'I'm sorry this was how you found out.'

Catherine's world was crumbling at her feet. Her body continued to tremble. Her jaw ached from how tightly she clenched it. All the once-proud knight could do was cry. Her knees weakened. She gripped her mother's pendant so hard the silver chain dug into her neck like a blunt saw.

Finally, she found her voice. 'Why… why was I not told this?'

'Your father didn't want you knowing the truth at all. He wouldn't tell me why, no matter how much I pushed him on it. He wanted you to remain in the dark about how she died until he decided the time was right and I don't think he'd ever talk to you about it.'

Catherine hugged herself, sniffling back tears. Her knees wobbled, threatening to buckle if she so much as swayed too much in one direction. The skin underneath her eyes were so puffy and irritated that closing them made them itch before more tears fell. She didn't know how to even begin processing what she'd learnt from Aldric.

Helena reached over and set her hand against Catherine's in a gentle attempt to bring her attention back to the present.

'Catherine, I've lived for over a century. I've felt what you're feeling many times. What I've realised is that emotions are human. That is how I tell the difference between a human and a monster. It sounds like your mother thought something similar too. A monster feels no remorse, no sorrow. You can still retain your humanity and be a vampire. Some vampires, like me, understand the threat that vampires like Erik pose to our kind and yours. I'm sure even other beings that were once human, like spirits, can still feel the same emotions before they weren't human anymore. It's okay to let yourself feel these conflicting feelings.'

Catherine slowly breathed in and out through her nose to slow her heart's rapid beating. She gave Helena the barest nod in response, still unable to speak. She sniffled and straightened her shoulders as if she could magically pull herself back together by doing so.

Aldric approached Catherine and patted her shoulder. 'I know it's a lot to take in, but I believe it is time that you learned the truth of what actually happened to your mother. She wanted to protect the people from vampires like Erik who only see them as cattle. Your mother was a lot like you in that regard.'

She looked up at the older knight, surprised.

'Yes, I know about Erik,' Aldric continued. 'Helena told me about him and I contracted her to kill him. Her hunting record was impressive, so I had no reason to believe she couldn't do it. Unfortunately, she caused quite a mess doing so and made the situation more complicated than it needed to be.'

Helena crossed her arms in front of her chest and bared her fangs at Aldric in frustration. 'I warned you that you'd need more than just me to bring him down, but did you listen? Of course not! Don't blame me and me alone for what happened. Unlike humans, vampires get stronger with age. I may be old to you, but he's much older and more powerful than me. You thought you knew better than the person he reawakened and supposedly loved but you don't.'

'Erik reawakened you?' Catherine muttered, shocked. She shook her head as the other part of Helena's outburst finally solidified in her mind. 'Wait, loved?!'

The vampire sighed and nodded reluctantly. 'Yes, and I don't want to go into it.'

'Helena,' Aldric started, sighing at the vampire's sudden eruption.

Helena's expression bore the mark of a woman whose skills had been dismissed and doubted one too many times. She pointed at Aldric, snarling.

'Don't even try it,' she snapped. 'I understand that all vampires seem equally powerful and scary to you mortals, but I refuse to have my talents diminished because you believed that I could defeat a vampire twice my age without assistance. You may think it perfectly acceptable to keep Catherine in the dark, but I, however, will not allow you to downplay the danger that Erik poses to human and undead alike.'

Catherine looked between Aldric and Helena, unsure of what to do or how to feel or even what to say.

'If you knew you'd struggle this much, why didn't you

tell me you couldn't handle it earlier?' Aldric asked.

Helena looked Aldric up and down, sneering with wounded pride. She looked over at Catherine, her face still dark with anger.

'I'm sorry you found out like this,' Helena said. 'Excuse me.'

She clenched her jaw and stormed past him, bumping his arm with her shoulder.

Aldric called after her.

Helena ignored him and slammed the door.

After the vampire left, Catherine felt a strange hollowness stake its claim in her chest as the silver cross' chill dissipated. She stared at the door, longing for Helena to return.

'Should I go after her?' Catherine asked, wiping away her tears.

'No,' Aldric replied. He smacked his lips together and patted Catherine's shoulder again. 'Give her some time to calm down first. I should've known better than to say what I did and keep you in the dark for so long. I hope you can find it in your heart to forgive me.'

Catherine nodded in silent understanding.

Though she heeded his words, Catherine didn't say anything. Her head swam with so many thoughts she swore the world span around her so fast, she wouldn't have been able to move without stumbling. Out of the seemingly endless questions that spawned in her mind, the ones about her mother remained at the forefront. She let her necklace fall from her fingers and clasped her hands.

Even if her gut feeling ended up being correct, she had to ask.

'Do you know if any of mother's research remains in her study?'

Aldric ran his hands over his face and through his hair, sighing as he thought back to the last time he'd been in that section of the manor. He stared up at the ceiling for a few seconds in silence.

'There's a chance. The Church requested all of her notes a long time ago, but she may have hidden a journal somewhere. Agnes was quite secretive from what I remember of her,' Aldric replied.

'Thanks,' Catherine said. 'Hopefully there's still something for me to find. It would be useful to have some of her research to fall back on. Maybe it'll help me feel close to her again?'

The older knight placed his hand on her shoulder and smiled at her sympathetically. 'I can't even imagine what it was like to grow up without your mother yet being old enough at the time to remember what she was like before her passing.'

While he meant well, his words stung. Catherine's eyes welled again and she wished that her body didn't have to produce so much sweat and tears. She sat down by her bed post and pulled her thighs close to her torso, wrapping her arms around her knees to keep herself from falling out of the ball she created. She rested her back against the post behind her and looked up at the ceiling above, avoiding Aldric's exhausted gaze. Her chest ached as her breaths shallowed.

A Knight's Blood

The moment he heard her sobs start up again, Aldric closed his eyes and scrunched his face.

'You don't need to go back to the Great Hall, you've had enough excitement for today,' Aldric said.

When he received no response from Catherine, he turned and left the room without another word.

As soon as the door closed behind him, much to her dismay, Catherine cried once again. Her eyes itched as she rubbed them with the side of her hand, sniffling back the mucus that trickled down from her nostrils. Everything was either irritated or sore from excessive crying and wounds not given the chance to fully heal. The weight of her thoughts crushed almost all of her willpower to continue. All she wanted to do was cry.

18

Once her thoughts became coherent again, Catherine picked herself up off the floor and washed her face at her washbasin, hoping cold water would dispel the mental fog that swept over her. Exhaustion plagued her waking moments since the tournament and refused to let go. The constant grief and stress hadn't helped.

Pushing through the brewing turmoil, Catherine decided she'd go check on Helena. Though she had no doubt Helena didn't need someone to regulate her emotional state, the knight wanted to get out of the manor. This just happened to be the most acceptable excuse she could think of.

The thought of being around the people who refused to tell her the truth until now enraged her more that she could explain. Just thinking of Erik playing nice with her liar of a father made her want to get violent.

Even if the voices that echoed from the Great Hall hours ago had faded to the barest of whispers, Catherine still didn't wish to run into nobles on her way out. If she were stopped, she knew she would have to answer tedious questions that would only serve to irritate her further.

Running into the knights her father favoured, knights like Robert, would do more than just irritate her. In fact, if Sir Badden dared to open his smarmy mouth she was certain that she'd lash out at him without a second thought. Just the thought of seeing him smirk made her hand twitch and involuntarily clench into a fist.

She needed to leave the manor. She needed to see Helena.

Having finally made up her mind, Catherine opened her bedroom door and crept through the corridor as quietly as she could to get to the stables undetected. Stealth was of the essence.

Sunset crept in through the windows before the night snuffed its brightness from the sky. The incoming light projected elongated diagonal shadows of the window panes they shone through. The shadows danced upon her body as she slunk through the corridors.

Her eyes were swollen and red from crying countless times during day. She pushed through the fatigue that nibbled at her heels, forcing herself forward when her muscles pleaded to stop.

The sorrow that refused to release its grip on her finally relented, allowing her rage to break free and take control.

Her brows furrowed. She clenched her teeth and her fists, ignoring the painful twinge in her jaw. No matter how she tried to calm herself, anger continued to run rampant through her head. Betrayal seeped back into her thoughts, further poisoning the memories of the earlier conversation with Aldric. She understood why he kept what he knew from her, but that didn't make it hurt any less.

Aldric's lack of transparency cut deep, tearing through her seemingly impenetrable trust in him as if it were nothing but linen. The man she relied on when Walter wasn't around, the man she saw as a father figure, proved himself as fickle as the men they teased behind closed doors. Memories of their interactions that she cherished prior took on a different hue. She doubted all he'd said to her over the years.

How could she judge whether he was honest with her in the past? Given all that had been revealed, what was true and what was said in order to "protect" her? How was keeping secrets about her mother's death protecting her?

Despite her sudden shift in perspective, she didn't blame the other knight. Not completely. Even if he had been acting in self-preservation as her enraged thoughts claimed, there had to be something, or someone, motivating said need for self-preservation.

Catherine stopped mid-step. Her rage-fuelled thoughts turned to the person truly responsible. The bone she had to pick wasn't with Aldric.

It was with Lord Geoffrey Seymour.

Her father was the one that forbade Aldric from physically helping her obtain the vampiric remains he asked for. Geoffrey was the one who held the education of Aldric's daughter over the older knight's head. It was him pushing Catherine to marry a nobleman. Geoffrey was the source of most of her strife and she couldn't do much about it. That made her despise him all the more.

Almost as if her anger willed her to confront him, Catherine stopped outside the door to her father's study. Her eyes widened as she placed her hand over her mouth, forcing herself to remain as silent as possible. No matter how she wanted to burst through the door and confront him, Catherine knew that it would only end badly for both of them. She held her breath and crept past her father's study on the tips of her toes, trying her very best to not make a sound.

A Knight's Blood

Her father's drunken mumblings were loud enough to slip through the crack underneath the door. Geoffrey's voice was unmistakable, but his words were so slurred that Catherine couldn't make out what he was saying without getting closer.

Catherine pushed her fury towards her father out of her mind and continued onward, eager to free herself from the prison her home was becoming. She didn't want to dwell on the man who decided long ago that she wasn't worth his time. Catherine was sure he didn't want to think about her unless absolutely necessary.

The knight stopped at the foot of the staircase two doorways down, feeling for her mother's necklace. She stared at the darkness that swallowed the stairs leading up to her mother's study. Longing bubbled up into her chest and overwhelmed the anger she dwelled on not even moments before.

Catherine hoped there were still secrets to be uncovered in that room, but she couldn't muster up the courage to climb that staircase. Not quite yet. She couldn't take another earth-shattering revelation. Not before she'd even processed what happened to her mother.

Catherine took her bodily response an indication that she should leave as quick as possible, lest she make the situation worse. She walked through the manor with purpose, eager to leave the manor grounds with the wind in her face upon Smokey's back.

She took a detour on her way to the stables and slipped into the kitchen, picking up a discarded sack and filling it with candles and a piece of flint to chase away the darkness in Helena's lair. Upon spying a plate of tarts left over, Catherine took one and put it in her mouth. She balanced the rest of the tart upon her lips as she hurried towards the stables, trying not to let the tart break before she could eat it.

Catherine finished off the tart she pilfered from the kitchen and tacked her horse in the stables, using the sunset's fleeting glow to properly see the buckles she fiddled with. She patted Smokey and cuddled his neck, smiling when he grumbled. She scratched behind his ear before she pulled herself up onto the saddle and grasped the reins.

With a click of her tongue and a tap of her heels, Smokey walked out of the stables. Once they were far enough from the manor grounds, she spurred him into a trot and then into a canter minutes later.

The knight and her steed headed down the road towards Birkstead and the old ruined church beyond the village as the sun fell below the horizon.

19

Catherine reached into her bag, pulling out the candles she brought with her. She sat them on one of the few tables that remained in the priest's chambers and lit their wicks with flint. She walked over to the open stone coffin in the centre of the room, wringing her hands.

The knight blew a nervous breath out of her lips. The majority of her tension left her body as she exhaled. Was she visiting the vampire too soon? Would Helena even talk to her after that argument between her and Aldric?

She slowly walked around the coffin, hugging herself. Catherine glanced into the coffin and stopped, staring at the woman sleeping peacefully inside.

Candlelight flickered over Helena's face, highlighting her aquiline nose, her lips, her cheeks, her jaw.

She was as serene as a statue. The shadows her nose cast over her cheek covered half of the tiny freckles dotting her skin. Helena hadn't gotten out of the dark green gown she'd worn earlier. The light from the candles made her sleeping form appear as if she were a fern on fire. She was so graceful, so beautiful.

She hadn't paid it any mind before, but seeing the vampire now in a green so reminiscent of her family's colours made the knight's heart swell. For just a moment, she let herself fantasise how enchanting the vampire would look in Seymour green and brown.

Gwendolyn K. Blackthorne

Catherine's mind wandered back to their kiss as her gaze lingered upon Helena's lips. She remembered how soft the vampire's lips were and swore they still ghosted upon her own. Her heart fluttered at the memory of how gentle Helena was.

She forced those thoughts from her mind, steeling herself to wake the vampire. The knight leant over the coffin, prodding Helena's shoulder with her finger.

The vampire didn't stir.

Catherine blew a stray hair away from her face and frowned. She prodded Helena's shoulder again, putting a little more force behind her poke.

The vampire's eyes flickered open. Her crimson irises glowed in the shadows surrounding the rest of her face. She leapt up and pressed Catherine against the wall, her fangs flashing in the candlelight. The distinct smell of copper clung to the vampire's teeth and fell upon the knight's face.

Catherine pulled her dagger from its sheath and held its sharp edge against Helena's arm before her fangs could descend upon her neck.

Helena let out a pained screech and stepped back. She held her hand over her scorched flesh. Searing pain flowed through her undead veins, forcing her to grit her teeth and hiss.

'What was that for?' the vampire demanded, glaring at the knight.

'You tried to tear my throat out,' Catherine replied, slowly lowering her dagger.

'What did you expect?' she retorted. 'You woke me up.'

Catherine sighed; she had reacted the same way when

the roles were reversed. She sheathed the dagger and offered Helena an apologetic smile.

The vampire rolled her eyes at the knight but smiled back at her. The hostility Helena had awoken with fell away the moment she saw Catherine's sheepish smile.

'You're right, I'm sorry about that.'

'I forgive you. You're lucky your blood tastes as good as it does,' Helena teased, tapping Catherine's nose with her finger. 'And that you're cute.'

Blood rushed to the knight's cheeks. She dipped her chin down towards her collarbone, trying to avoid looking at Helena. Swallowing what little saliva coating her tongue, Catherine wriggled out of Helena's weakening grasp but her back remained against the wall. Her pulse danced faster as panicked thoughts swam through her mind.

The most beautiful woman she'd ever seen said she was cute.

Taking a moment to unsuccessfully steady herself, the knight cleared her throat. 'I wanted to ask you some more questions. And see if you were well after what happened with Aldric.'

Helena quirked an eyebrow at Catherine. 'I'm fine, just a little hurt by his lack of trust and confidence in my abilities, that's all. As to your questions, I suppose fair is fair. I'll answer your questions, provided I get some of your blood in return. Silver inflicted wounds don't heal themselves.'

Helena let her gaze linger on Catherine's exposed neck, her tongue playfully poking between her teeth.

'If you try to drink too much, I shall run you through,'

189

Catherine said, setting her hand on her dagger to hammer home her threat.

'That's reasonable,' Helena agreed.

The vampire's sharp canines gave her mischievous grin the dangerous edge that thrilled Catherine whenever she caught a glimpse of it.

Helena jumped onto the nearest table and sat back against the mossy stone wall, examining a nearby candle.

The knight lounged against the wall, resting her hands on her hips as she bent her knees and slid down onto the floor.

'What made you leave a life of nobility?' Catherine asked.

'Went straight for a hard one, didn't you?'

The vampire's glee waned. She sighed. The fire that made her so charismatic and enchanting dimmed as she stared at the wall behind the knight.

'Very well. It hurts to remember now, but there was once a time as a mortal I thought I had some control over my fate. I spent a year getting the knight I fancied to teach me to use a sword, just as an excuse to be close to him. He was beautiful, but obsessed with obtaining things and people no one else could have. Because he had my attention and my affection, something I didn't give to anyone else, he was willing to spend time with me. I even "ruined my reputation" for him. Mother's words, not mine.' Helena rolled her eyes and continued. 'I never saw it that way. I still don't understand how enthusiastic intimacy could be bad thing. I thought I was going to marry him and we were going to have a happy family together. I was naïve enough to believe

I could have that.'

Helena's expression hardened as she recollected memories of her mortal life and spoke them aloud. Her gaze refused to meet Catherine's.

It seemed as if no matter how many years had passed, there was still something human about her; something soft and vulnerable.

The knight wished to reach out and comfort Helena, but didn't. She watched in silence as an unholy being in possession of divine abilities descended into emotions they thought had been shed along with their mortality. Catherine said nothing and let Helena continue.

'I was rudely awakened to reality when he married the woman I considered my best friend. Our lessons stopped immediately and she rubbed the fact they were married in my face every time I saw her. My heart couldn't take the torture, so I stole the sword father had commissioned for his time as a Templar Knight and ran away from home. That was when I met Erik and his coven. I didn't know they were vampires at first. I thought they were just bandits. Erik took a shining to me, and before I knew it, I had fallen for his brutish charisma.'

The knight scrunched her nose and lips with disgust.

Helena saw Catherine's expression and burst out into a fit of giggles, pulling her out of her sombre mindset for a moment. 'What? Don't look at me like that. I know I have a type.'

'What made Erik so interesting anyway?' Catherine asked.

'He was in Ireland at the time because he was on a

191

Viking and couldn't get on the boat back to Denmark. Erik told me it was because he would have to drain everyone on board in order to survive in the sun. I believed him at the time, but now I'm not so sure.'

'Don't give me details of your relationship with him, just tell me what happened after he reawakened you,' the knight pleaded, holding her hands up in surrender.

The vampire rolled her eyes again and swept some of her hair in front of her shoulder. She stroked a lock of hair as she continued her story. 'It was soon after I realised I liked him that he guided me through the reawakening process. It took two days, but I was finally a vampire like the rest of them. As quickly as I came to feel for him, those emotions left. He did something that disgusted me and I could not bring myself to see past it.'

'Well? What happened?'

'I'm getting there. This all happened a hundred years ago. Anyway, everything was great until Erik decided that a rival coven was a threat. They were vampires like us, but he wanted to slaughter them as if they were nothing but swine. That coven was much smaller than us and didn't even hunt in the same part of the country as we did, but he thought they wanted to destroy us. Some of his band, myself included, thought he was being paranoid. We voiced our concerns and he lost his mind. Because I had his affection, my transgressions weren't as harshly punished, but I was punished all the same. He had to send a message to the others, after all.'

Catherine stared at Helena in disbelief. Her mouth hung open for a moment before she asked, 'What did he do?'

'To scare us into submission, Erik had two of his best

men chained to trees and left them there so the sun could slowly burn them alive. It was horrific. We couldn't help them without suffering either. Our archer tried to free them and had his head torn from his body. It took days for those two men to die. Their skin was peeling from their bodies before they perished. Their bodies couldn't heal their wounds quick enough because they hadn't fed. I couldn't stand to look at him after he had me dispose of their corpses. They would have no grave marker or even a grave. I had to throw them into a bog in the middle of the day so I would burn and blister in the sun but wouldn't die like they had. Erik was a monster. He revelled in the pain and horror he'd inflicted upon us. He craved the fear he inspired in us.'

Catherine got to her knees and crawled a little closer to the table Helena had claimed as her seat.

'Why didn't you kill him back then?' the knight asked.

Helena pursed her lips and closed her eyes, breathing in a breath she didn't need. Her chest shuddered as she repressed the memories of the horrors Erik had put other vampires through. She opened her eyes and looked over at Catherine, giving the knight a small, saddened smile. The vampire shook her head, trying to keep her lip from quivering.

'I wasn't strong enough at the time. I had just left the fledgling stage and had no idea how to use my new abilities properly. For the second time in my life, I was helpless. Couldn't stand feeling that way. I was desperate and I chose to run away from my problems yet again. Without telling anyone my plans, I fled to Greece. My time in Athens is a whole other story, but to keep it short, I spent time working with a group of vampires who hunted those of us who caused havoc and grew into who I am today. Helena isn't my real name; it was one I was given by my fellow hunters and I liked it enough to keep it.'

Catherine stared at Helena in wonder. Some of the chest-tightening awe she felt when she first saw the woman at the tournament returned. The vampire's strength never ceased to amaze her. 'I can't believe all of that happened to you. It sounds insane.'

'You'd be surprised how much occurs within a century,' Helena replied, shrugging with amusement at the knight's words. 'But now you know why I fought Erik that night and why I've been waiting for the right moment to strike after then. It's also why I didn't want to sugar coat how dangerous Erik is. Bravado can be a dangerous thing; it has killed many a vampire and mortal before and will continue to do so.'

She gave Helena a small supportive smile. 'Thank you. I'm tired of being deceived and appreciate your honesty.'

Silence drifted over the two of them but refused to cloak them in the chilliness that often came with it. Flickering flames danced upon their wicks, throwing their yellowed light around the room. They gazed at each other, quietly acknowledging the warmth simmering between them.

Helena crossed her ankles and leant back on her hands, smiling at Catherine as her sorrow faded into the back of her mind. The vampire's shoulders fell away from her jaw, the weight of her past falling away for the time being. A smirk stretched across her plump pink lips and awakened the mischievous twinkle that usually appeared in her striking eyes.

'I forgot to tell you that the story comes at an extra cost,' Helena teased, winking at the knight.

Catherine quirked an eyebrow. 'Let me guess, more blood?'

'A generous offer, however, I don't want to get stuck

by that knife again.'

'Then what do you want?' Catherine asked.

'How about a kiss?'

The breath Catherine had just taken got caught in her throat. Her eyes widened. Excitement bubbled in her belly. Once more, Catherine swallowed what little saliva covered her tongue, dislodging the breath that was stuck. The kiss in the manor's chapel replayed in her mind, sending shivers dancing along her arms and down her spine. She opened and closed her mouth, trying to piece together her answer and failing to do so. The sensation of simply pressing her lips together and parting them repeatedly only served to fluster her more. Warmth spread across Catherine's cheeks and pooled between her thighs as she thought of kissing Helena again.

Words failed her, so Catherine simply nodded in reply.

The vampire's smirk widened as she leant forward, placing her hands on her knees to keep herself from falling from the table. Her crimson irises roamed up and down Catherine's body, settling on her flushed face.

'Use your words,' Helena commanded, quirking her eyebrow at the knight. 'I want to hear you tell me you want a kiss.'

Catherine's mouth hung open as Helena's words stopped her racing thoughts in their tracks. She licked her lips and sat up straighter, meeting the copper-haired beauty's hungry gaze with her own pleading one. Tingles ran through her body as she recognised that Helena's hunger wasn't purely for blood.

'Please, kiss me.'

'That's more like it,' the vampire cooed, smirking wider.

195

Helena jumped down from the table and got on her hands and knees. Her hair fell onto her shoulders as she arched her back and slunk over to Catherine.

The knight remained still. Her heart throbbed so violently she was sure it was going to leap into her throat and out of her mouth for Helena to catch and cradle. Catherine watched how Helena crawled across the stone floor towards her, captivated by how gracefully the vampire moved. She folded her knees underneath her body, placing her hands upon her thighs and squaring her shoulders. Anticipation stiffened her spine and constricted her ribs as she held her breath. When Helena was within arm's reach, Catherine held her arms out towards her. Her pulse quickened, excited to have the other woman close again.

Without saying a word, Helena glanced up at Catherine from underneath her lashes. She placed her forearms on the knight's shoulders, laying one hand on top of the other, avoiding getting burnt by the silver chain around Catherine's neck. The vampire's fingers grasped the loosened sections of the knight's dark hair, pulling her braid ever so gently.

Catherine's scalp prickled as her head followed the weight of Helena's hand, tilting her chin upward to expose her neck. Her eyes flickered closed and a moan fell from her lips. A breath tremored in her throat, the chill from her necklace coaxing goosebumps from her flesh.

As soon as the thought appeared, Catherine felt a show of trust was necessary. Helena had done so by telling her story, Catherine wanted to return the favour.

She reluctantly moved her hands away from the vampire kneeling in front of her and removed the chain from her neck. The cross was placed into her pocket, safe and sound. Her neck felt bare without it hanging against her collarbone. The goosebumps it coaxed from her skin began to dissipate, leaving only the bruises and scabs from the days before behind.

The vampire let go of Catherine's hair and stared at her, surprised. A smile touched her lips as she hummed with delight. Helena pressed her wrists against the back of Catherine's neck, revelling in skin-to-skin contact without pain.

Catherine opened her eyes and glanced up at Helena, meeting the vampire's gaze. Her cheeks remained flushed by the blood pulsing through her body. She placed her hands on Helena's hips, silently admiring how utterly delicious she felt to touch. Undeath clearly hadn't affected how soft her body was. She rubbed her thumbs in circles in the dips of Helena's back, relishing in the sighs that she coaxed from the vampire.

Without warning, Helena straddled Catherine's hips, wrapping her legs around her. She pressed her body against the knight's, positioning her lips just in front of Catherine's. Helena pulled a hand away from her neck and caressed the other woman's cheek, running the tips of her fingers along the knight's jaw.

Catherine felt the ghost of Helena's lips brush hers and leant closer, chasing the tantalising taste of the vampire's mouth. She whined as Helena pulled away the moment their lips touched.

The vampire chuckled at Catherine's scrunched nose and impatient sigh. She felt the blood surge through Catherine's body, thumping in her veins. She wriggled upon the knight's lap, teasing her more whilst getting comfortable. Helena used the hand cradling Catherine's cheek to guide the knight's lips towards hers.

Helena kissed Catherine.

The feeling of Helena's cold soft lips against her own

threw her off balance. Catherine's back shuddered as excitement violently and passionately flooded her thoughts. Even with the vampire sitting upon her lap, the world around her span so wildly that Catherine had to tense her stomach to stay in place. Catherine's hands tightened around Helena's hips, pulling her as close as she possibly could to ground herself.

Growing up, Catherine always thought that the kisses the girls around her whispered about were exaggerated to garner attention from their fellows. Never in her wildest dreams had she thought their tittering about magical kisses would be anything close to the truth. And yet, she was proven wrong.

This kiss was so much better than the last. Catherine mentally scolded herself for believing that their little peck in the chapel was as close to Heaven as she'd get on earth.

This moment with the vampire was utter bliss.

Helena's caresses left tingles trailing across Catherine's cheek and neck, coaxing goosebumps from her flesh. Her touches were slow and methodical. She gently suckled Catherine's bottom lip, eliciting a surprised gasp from the knight. Helena's fangs pressed into her lip without breaking her skin.

Catherine sighed, her shoulders slumping as Helena broke the kiss. She slowly opened her eyes to find the vampire doing the same. The knight's hands remained on the vampire's hips, keeping Helena in place upon her lap. A smile touched her lips. Warmth bloomed in her chest before it radiated through the rest of her body.

'You didn't come here just to listen to me speak about my past and kiss me, did you?' Helena teased, tilting her head to the side and grinning at the red-faced knight.

Catherine glanced down at the ground, wide-eyed as

reality came back into focus. 'Ah… you're right,' she said, stumbling over her words. 'That kiss was really good.'

The vampire chuckled. 'I'm glad you liked it.'

She cleared her throat, reminding herself that she came here for a reason. Catherine tried her best to ignore the fact that Helena remained on her lap and licked her lips as she pieced together her questions.

'Are there any other ways to protect the village from vampires? Other than becoming a vampire or enlisting the help of one?'

'There's not a lot you can do, honestly. Sure, we're weak to hawthorn, yew, and silver, but that doesn't ward us away. Wounds created by those materials take longer to heal and requires blood to kickstart the healing process. Holy water isn't going to do much either, obviously,' Helena explained, gesturing at the ruined church and, by extension, the consecrated grounds she called her lair. 'You can have a group of humans dedicated to staving off vampires, but their numbers will dwindle due to fear and death. Or, you could have a vampire protect the village. Believe it or not, there are others like me that can be contracted to kill the unrulier vampires. Naturally, you'd have to pay and it may not be purely monetary, but we're the best option for a reason. Sure, we'll struggle against older vampires, like how a squire would struggle against a fully-fledged knight. I'm sorry, those are your only options to protect people long-term.'

Catherine couldn't help but sigh; she really had hoped that there was something else she could do. 'And that's why Aldric had been contracting you in secret?'

Helena nodded. 'Yes. I highly doubt he would tell his liege, your father, that he was doing so. Don't think he'd like he'd like that very much.'

Catherine scoffed and rolled her eyes. 'You're right about that. He doesn't like anything that costs him money or would isolate him from his friends.'

The vampire got off the knight's lap. She stroked the side of Catherine's face with a sad yet understanding smile. 'Like I said, bravado can be a dangerous thing.'

'Well, I don't know what I expected but at least I know the options now,' Catherine replied with a frown. 'How are fledglings made?'

'Reawakening is a very painful process,' Helena explained. Though she had no need to breathe, her shoulders slumped as if she sighed. 'Adjusting to the new changes can take a long time once the fledgling reawakens. The process begins when a vampire drains a human of blood and gives the human a few drops of vampiric blood in return. I was "dead" for two days before I reawakened, though it can happen within a day, like Walter. The first five months are always the hardest. During this time the magic that allows us to function after death is working the hardest it ever will. You're going to be thirsty every day. You can drink animal blood, though it won't sustain you the same way human blood does. Bloodlust will be quite strong for those five months. It'll be all you think about. Even the most moral of people don't care if they have to feed off a horse twice or thrice a day. One human's worth of blood will be enough to satiate a fledgling for a day. It's not the volume that counts. The magic that adjusts the body to undeath works quicker with human blood than animal blood, it's something to do with how potent the soul is.'

'It certainly does sound like a painful experience,'

Catherine commented, grimacing at the thought of undergoing such a trial.

'Oh, it is,' Helena replied. 'It's not something I'd recommend going into without knowing what you're in for.'

'I got lucky against Walter, that much is true. I don't believe for a moment I would survive an encounter with Erik without someone like you by my side,' Catherine admitted. 'If you've struggled to take him down and you're faster and stronger than me, then there isn't a hope in Heaven that I could do so alone.'

Helena jumped back onto the table.

Catherine's sapphire eyes darted back and forth, as if she were watching something fly around in the almost complete darkness above them. Calloused hands stroked the hilt of her weapon, itching for a fight. The longer she sat in silence, the more of her fleeting ideas became pieces falling into place to solve the puzzle in her head.

Erik and Helena had a history. Erik also getting rather friendly with her father. If he wanted to ensure that Birkstead became his hunting ground, he had to kill Helena and try to convince Catherine's father to marry her to him, which Catherine would fight against to the bitter end.

Maybe, like Helena had joked when they first spoke about taking Erik down, Catherine was the best bait available? Maybe he'd want to confront the two of them to keep Catherine away from the ex-lover who would expose his plan?

'You're planning something, aren't you?' Helena asked.

'I've been tasked to kill two vampires within a week, after which I will be married off to someone my father chooses.

If I survive that long, that is. I have to plan or I will be lost,' she replied, her small smile falling from her lips.

The vampire bared her fangs in a devious smile. 'It's been a long time since I've heard wisdom like that from a human. Aldric told me about that task the day you were given it. I suppose he wanted to help without being pegged by your father as actually helping. I know what it's like to have a parent treat you like they're selling the prized calf and the more I got to know you, the more I didn't want you to go through that too.'

She smiled at Helena, feeling the warmth from before rekindle within her chest. 'Thanks, I appreciate it.'

'If you're going after Erik, you're going to need some help. And not from other humans.'

'Are you offering?' the knight asked, an impulsive twinge of glee colouring her voice.

'To finally put Erik in his place? Of course,' Helena replied.

'Very well. One must strike while the iron is hot. Do you think he'd show up if we went down to Birkstead tonight?'

'There's always a chance. He needs to feed sometime and I doubt he'd do so in your manor. It echoes in there and there's too many people around. One scream will draw the attention of almost everyone there and he won't like that.'

Helena slipped down from the table. She sauntered over to Catherine's side once more and placed her hands on either side of the knight, trapping her between her and the wall. She looked down upon Catherine with a lopsided smirk as Catherine squirmed underneath her gaze.

A Knight's Blood

'You got what you wanted, now it's time to uphold your end of the deal,' Helena said.

Catherine looked up at Helena's smirk, giddy chills sweeping down her back.

'You've trusted me to tell you the truth, now you have to trust me,' Helena teased.

The vampire bent down and licked the side of Catherine's throat, savouring how her skin felt against her tongue. Helena moved her hand from the wall to the side of Catherine's neck. The rapid pulsing of Catherine's veins excited her more than she could vocalise.

Catherine drew in a breath and held it. She grasped the hilt of the silver dagger tighter. She winced as Helena's fangs punctured her neck. She closed her eyes and hissed as Helena's fingernails dug into the back of her neck. Warmth flooded her body as the vampire moaned tasting her blood. Electricity danced along Catherine's skin, setting her whole body alight. An intoxicating concoction of excitement, fear, and desire gripped her, forcing her to arch her back to get closer to Helena.

'Helena…' Catherine uttered, sighing.

The second the vampire's name left the knight's lips, Helena bit down harder.

A gasp wavered from Catherine's lips as Helena's tongue swished across the punctures she'd created. Catherine's hands ran up and down Helena's back. She grasped the vampire's hips, digging her nails into her flesh. Though she was perfectly still, everything around her span as if she were freefalling.

Helena pulled away from Catherine's neck, catching the

knight as she collapsed into her arms. She cradled Catherine against her chest, running her hand down her dark hair.

'You okay?' Helena asked, keeping her voice low and gentle.

'Yeah. I don't think it's the blood loss, just overwhelmed,' Catherine replied. The world around her continued spinning even with her eyes wide open. Vibrations from Helena's humming soothed her racing mind. 'So much has happened in such a short time, it's hard to parse what's passed and what's to come.'

Before Catherine could even come to her senses completely, Helena tilted her head up.

She licked away the blood that settled in the crevasses in her lips, ensuring that not a single drop remained.

Catherine couldn't take another breath before Helena pressed her lips against hers. Her knees weakened as the kiss stole whatever air remained in her lungs. The bite steadily throbbed on the side of her neck, pain fuelling her desire for the woman kissing her.

Helena pulled away and gazed down at Catherine, smiling at how blissful she looked. Helena dipped her head below the knight's jaw and peppered the sensitive skin around the fresh bite with kisses. She slowly pulled away to give the knight some room to breathe.

'You might want to sit for a while,' the vampire whispered.

Catherine nodded slowly in understanding.

Never in her life had she expected to befriend a vampire,

let alone allow one to touch her in such a sensual and intimate way. And yet, it was the only thing in her life that felt right.

20

The night air swept through Birkstead. It caressed the back of Catherine's neck, coaxing goosebumps from her flesh where her necklace's chill could not.

The moon shone brightly against the darkness above. Stars twinkled in the night sky like scattered diamonds in firelight. Pale, white light illuminated the village as the last few windows were closed, dimming the warm glow from fireplaces. Serenity descended upon the village like a parent draping a blanket over a sleeping child. The occasional bleating of the sheep out in the field broke the silence but didn't disturb the peace.

Catherine loved watching the hustle and bustle of everyday life in Birkstead. That didn't stop her from enjoying the village's tranquillity at night. Her evening patrols used to be the highlight of her week, even more so when she got to share them with Walter or Aldric. Since Walter's death, that tranquillity she once relished sent shivers down her spine. Dread bubbled in the back of her mind as the silver necklace's chill continued to make her skin crawl.

Gravel crunched underneath their boots as the two women walked through Birkstead together, side by side. Catherine had to move slightly faster in order to keep up with Helena, her height and undead speed making her strides much longer than Catherine's. Though they didn't exchange words, they stole glances, smiling when they caught each other's eye.

A Knight's Blood

Catherine kept her hand on the pommel of her sword, appreciating the weight of it upon her belt and her shield against her arm once again. Her weapons gave her the power and control she wished she had over the rest of her life. The corner of her shield struck her chainmail as she strode beside the vampire, clinking with almost every step. With her sword and her shield, Catherine could take on the world.

The tiny sound of metal striking metal coaxed a small chuckle from Helena. 'You mortals and your need for elaborate protection. Any vampire could hear you from the other side of the village without needing to pay attention.'

Rolling her eyes and shaking her head with a snort, Catherine nudged Helena with her elbow.

'That's a little hypocritical. Didn't you wear a full set of armour in the tournament?' Catherine asked.

'I needed to fit in and protect my skin from the sun. I didn't wear it for protection against weapons. My body heals quickly enough on its own to negate the need for armour,' Helena replied.

'Unfortunately, I need to wear armour so I don't die easily in battle. I can't take a sword through the chest and survive, let alone survive without suffering long term injuries.'

'Doesn't change the fact you still heal a little faster than any other human I've met. Not incredibly so, but you still heal a little faster than most,' she pointed out. 'Or that you can see through vampiric glamours.'

The knight hummed with uncertainty. She ran her fingers over the scabbed punctures on her neck and sighed. 'While I'm as curious as you are to know why, we should deal with one issue at a time. Let's focus on finding Erik first.'

Helena nodded. 'You're right. I'm sure we'll figure out why you can do what you can do in time.'

'In time,' Catherine echoed.

Despite the fact that she was there to find and kill Erik, Catherine couldn't help but glance at Helena every now and again. Even in the dark, she could still make out the outlines of Helena's muscles, the sway of her hips, the curve of her jaw. The moon's pale glow danced upon her features and made her appear as if she were made of stone. Catherine couldn't help but to find herself enamoured with the vampire and how she made herself appear so delicate in social settings but so dangerous when combat was inevitable.

The moon's light was so bright a halo caressed its edge. While its glow illuminated some of the world around her, it wasn't anywhere near bright enough to let her see her surroundings clearly. Catherine stared up at the stars, trying her hardest not to let her thoughts overwhelm her.

Conflicting feelings battled for dominance. Admiration and adoration warmed her chest and stole some of her breath as she caught a glimpse of Helena's luscious lips.

She forced her attention to return to the task at hand: hunting Erik.

The two women continued walking, approaching the building Helena and Erik had destroyed during their fight earlier in the week.

Catherine stopped beside one of the collapsed walls and examined the chapel. Though shadows obscured most of the remaining debris, she didn't need the light to know that all the damaged furniture had been removed. Catherine had been there when the furniture was being cleared. She crept closer, lifting her shield to guard the left side of her torso. The knight's sword screeched against its sheath as she pulled it from its resting place and held it by her side, pointing the tip towards the ground.

Memories of the night the chapel was destroyed flashed in the darkness behind her eyes when she blinked. Shivers ran through her body as she froze in panic. Catherine let out an elongated breath to calm her racing heart.

It wasn't going to be like that night.

She was with Helena.

A large stone bounced across the chapel's stone floor.

Helena's head turned towards the broken building. The vampire stared at the debris and then over at Catherine.

'What is it?' Catherine asked.

'I hear something.'

Helena tentatively talked towards the building, lifting her chin and sniffing the air to see if she could pin down what made that stone move. She caught a whiff of blood and damp earth coming from near the knight. The tip of her sword trailed behind her, carving her path back to where Catherine stood. She narrowed her eyes and scanned the area carefully, ensuring nothing would take her by surprise.

A breeze blew through Birkstead, chilling Catherine as the air brushed her neck.

Helena, thanks to her undead nature, was unaffected by

any change in temperature.

The vampire could hear everything happening around them, but Catherine could only hear the wind's whistling and the distant bleating of sheep.

Anticipation bubbled in the pit of Catherine's stomach. Because her mortal eyesight didn't allow her to see what the vampire could, she watched the woman's gaze and expression to gauge if something was hiding amongst the rubble. In times like these, she wished that she had heightened senses like Helena's.

The vampire lifted the tip of her sword away from the ground and held it firmly out in front of her. A frown hardened her beautiful face into a ferocious mask of war. She licked her lips and revealed her fangs in a half-snarl.

The shift in the vampire's demeanour told the knight she had found the threat they were looking for. Catherine shifted her feet, widening her stance and bending her knees so she could leap into battle beside Helena.

'Don't be shy, Erik,' Helena said, her voice low and vicious. 'Come out and play.'

A deep laugh echoed, bouncing around what remained of the chapel's stone walls. The figure swaggered over to the opening in the wall, swinging their axe over their shoulder with a bloodthirsty smirk. Blond braids trailed down their shoulders. Dark warpaint was smeared over their eyes and across their face. Red eyes pierced through the darkness. The wicked axe glinted in the moonlight, the steel glowing as if it were made of starlight.

'Back again, are we?' Erik asked, grinning at Helena before shifting his gaze towards Catherine. 'And you brought me a snack. How thoughtful.'

A Knight's Blood

'You're not going to feed from her,' Helena spat in reply. 'I won't allow it.'

Erik lifted his axe off his shoulder and held it down by his side, shifting his feet with a chuckle. The blond vampire tilted his head to the side and shook his head at them both. He took a step towards Helena, glaring at her incredulously. 'You won't allow it? You have no say in what I do. You answer to me.'

'Not anymore,' Helena said. The vampire glared back at him, refusing to break eye contact. 'You may have reawakened me, but I don't answer to you. I never will again. You lost that privilege when I left you and your coven behind.'

'And you left me to flit through different social circles looking for someone like you. Mortal social circles. For someone who's lived a hundred years, you'd know by now that predators don't mingle with prey,' he said, baring his fangs. 'They kill them.'

'Only barbarians believe there is no tact in social warfare. If all you care about is the kill, why haven't you gorged yourself already?' Helena questioned, sneering at her ex-lover.

'Though I never cared much for it in Ireland, the Church's bounty on vampiric remains continues to be a pain here in England. While it makes the weak bold, it encourages them to band together. There's only so much silver a vampire can take. And yet, I feel this village would be perfect as a haven for myself and the new coven I'll create. Birkstead would make a great stronghold. It even comes with its own little farm,' Erik answered.

Catherine's eyes widened. Lines wracked her forehead as she clenched her teeth. She glared at him from underneath her browbone as if her gaze alone could melt the flesh from his bones. Blood and rage pulsed through her veins with the fury of a thousand hounds. Her grip on her sword tightened.

Helena glanced at Catherine, concern softening her expression. She reached out to the knight, barely touching her shoulder as Catherine stepped past her.

The knight stopped in front of Helena, raising her shield in case Erik lunged. Catherine lifted her sword and pointed the tip at Erik, clutching the hilt as if it were his throat.

'I'd rather die than allow my people to become cattle for monsters like you!'

The blond vampire raised an eyebrow at Catherine. 'Monsters like me? Be careful what you say, little knight. I made the woman behind you a "monster like me".'

'I'm not like you, Erik,' Helena said, shaking her head at the other vampire. Her fangs were still on full display. 'I don't slaughter peasants for fun or leave vampires to die in the sun over simple disagreements. I will, however, take great pleasure in ensuring you suffer before I rip your heart from your chest and make eating it the last thing you ever see.'

He beat his chest with his fist and playfully pouted. He dropped his hand and his act a moment later. He stepped closer to Catherine, staring at her. Erik turned to Helena, grinning.

'Aoibheann, the only heart that will be eaten tonight is that of your little pet,' Erik replied, cocking his head towards the knight.

Before Catherine could speak, Helena sped around her and stopped in the space between the knight and the other vampire.

She pressed the tip of her sword into the ground in front

of Catherine's shield. Helena's face was centimetres from Erik's, her expression stormy.

'You will not touch her,' Helena hissed. 'And you will never call me that again!'

The two vampires glared at each other, barely moving a muscle. Decades of bad blood simmered between them, ready to boil over at any second.

'Is that your best threat?' Erik asked, chuckling at Helena's fury. 'Do the two of you really think you'd stand a chance fighting me? You were always the weakest and she's only human.'

Catherine gritted her teeth. The pounding of her head heart drowned out all logic and replaced it with near-blind rage. She glared at Erik, listening to the thoughts that screeched for his demise.

The smiling vampire took Walter from her. He turned her mentor into the monster he despised becoming. Nothing would stop Catherine from putting Erik down and taking his fangs.

Erik had to be destroyed.

Unable to hold herself back any longer, Catherine lunged out from behind Helena and swung at Erik.

The blond stepped back faster than Catherine could follow.

Her sword cut through the pelt that hung from his waist, missing his body completely.

Erik moved to attack Catherine, but Helena was faster. Her longsword caught his axe as she surged forward and clashed with him. She tilted her sword upward to lock his weapon with hers to try and disarm him.

He unhooked his axe from her blade. A guttural growl left his lips as he raised his weapon and bared his fangs, swinging at her.

Helena wove underneath his axe's arc and kicked him in the stomach, sending him stumbling backwards into one of the chapel's weakened stone walls.

The impact of his back against the wall cracked some of the remaining mortar, sending smaller stones skittering across the chapel's tiles as he fell to a knee.

Erik whipped his head up, loose hair and braids flying around his face and snarling at his former lover. The blond vampire launched back onto his feet, sprinting for Helena with his axe raised high. He swung downwards, the blade cutting Helena's thigh as she barely dodged out of the way.

Helena hissed, glancing at the tear in her pants. Blood trickled from her new wound, staining the brown fabric. She shifted her stance, attempting to keep her weight off that leg until it healed enough for her to use it effectively again.

Catherine saw Erik raise his axe to strike Helena again and leapt in to intercept the blow. She thrust her shield up as his axe came down, forcing it to bounce off her shield with an echoing clang. Without pausing to catch her breath, she pushed forward, slamming the shield into Erik's chest with all her might.

His back hit the wall and Catherine thrust her sword into his side, twisting her now-bloodied blade to pin him in place.

Erik screamed as the tip of Catherine's sword carved through his flesh and scraped bone. He wriggled his arms up from his sides, contorting his arm around the sword to avoid dropping his axe. His nose and forehead crinkled once his hands were free and he found purchase against her shield. Flattening his back against the wall behind him, he shoved Catherine off him.

The knight's grip on her sword weakened and she fell backward, hitting the ground with a thud. A yelp fell from her lips as pain shot through back. The back of her head prickled and ached from smacking the gravel. Catherine winced, stretching her fingers and noting the loss of her sword. She sat up and watched as Erik pulled her sword from his body and tossed it to the side.

She stared at her main weapon as it skipped across the gravel with a clatter. Catherine's heart stopped as his blazing red eyes settled on her. She scrambled to her feet, stumbling backward when she lost her balance. Fear grasped her thoughts and held them tight just as her saliva dried up.

Erik barely had the chance to step away from the crumbling chapel wall before he was forced to the ground once more.

Helena ran at Erik, ramming her sword into his stomach. She took advantage of the moment he doubled over and punched him in the face.

His cheekbone crumpled with a sickening crack.

The power and anger she put behind the punch sent Erik crashing into the wall.

Whatever mortar left to hold the wall together shattered when Erik fell through the wall. The loosened stones crashed down upon him. Dust swirled up into the air, dancing as if all that stirred it was the wind.

215

The chilling bite of the night air stole any smell Catherine would've been able to detect. Her nostrils prickled as she inhaled to slow her speeding heart. Sweat trickled down her back, forcing shivers to dance along her spine.

Though Catherine couldn't detect it, Helena was acutely aware of how the fresh scent of copper and decay overpowered the earthy ones she'd associated with Birkstead. Thankfully, no one in the houses behind them stirred loud enough that her vampiric hearing could pick up. The last thing they needed was for some curious mortals to become collateral.

The knight's sword scraped against the gravel with a shrill grating shriek as she picked it up. Catherine adjusted her grip, tightening her hold on the hilt so her blade wouldn't be taken from her again. Her head throbbed harder and faster than her blood pumped through her body. A wave of dizziness swept over her, but she shook it off.

Helena wandered over to Catherine's side, pressing the tip of her sword down into the ground and leaning on it as a crutch. She bit back a whimper. Despite the fact it still bled, the cut on her thigh began to knit itself together. Helena patted Catherine's shoulder, smiling back at her.

Helena's smile dropped.

A stone skittered across the ground, stopping mere centimetres from Helena's feet.

She turned towards the rubble. A pair of pebbles tumbled from the top. Her expression hardened. She swept the tip of her blade away from the gravel, pressing the flat of the sword against her back.

'What is it?' Catherine asked.

'Stand back,' Helena instructed, glancing over her

216

shoulder at Catherine. 'There's a chance he'll jump straight for you if you're too close.'

Catherine stared at the rubble, stepping backward as it trembled. The knight raised her shield, holding it in front of her head and shoulders.

Erik burst from the debris, dust and rocks flying in all directions. Fangs on full display, he brandished his axe with a flourish and bellowed a war cry.

Stones rained down upon Catherine and bounced off her shield, skipping across the ground before her. She lowered her shield the moment stones stopped clattering.

Erik launched himself at Helena before the dust had even settled, tackling her to the gravel. He straddled her waist and held his axe up to strike.

Catherine ran to Helena's side, shield up and sword at the ready. Her heart stopped and her feet refused to as she watched Erik bury his axe into Helena's chest over and over, smirking every time his ex-lover cried out in pain. She pushed back the tears that formed upon seeing the woman she cared for hurt. Anger surged through her veins, pushing her to move faster. The knight dug her feet into the gravel, stopping beside the wrestling vampires. She swung her sword at Erik, screaming with frustration when he caught the blade with one hand.

Blood trickled down his palm as he gripped her sword tighter, keeping her from striking again.

Catherine slammed her shield into the back of Erik's head, hoping that the blow would force him to release her weapon. Much to her disappointment, he cried out but refused to let go. She switched tactics and tugged her sword as hard as she could, wondering if there was enough blood to let the blade slip from his fingers.

Despite the pain, Helena clenched her jaw and plunged her longsword into his stomach. Venomous glee spread across her face as it became Erik's turn to suffer. She forced the blade to carve its way through his body, grimacing as it fought to pierce through bone.

Catherine's shield collided with Erik's head once more, forcing a sickening crack to echo through Birkstead.

For a moment, his eyelids fluttered closed and his body shuddered from the impact. His eyes snapped open again, his red irises blazing with bloodlust. Erik released Catherine's sword, forcing her to stagger backwards. He yanked his axe from Helena's chest, running his tongue across his teeth as she screamed.

'Fear always looked good on you,' Erik muttered, placing the edge of his axe against her throat.

Helena's crimson irises glimmered. She scrunched her nose and bared her fangs. She adjusted her grip on her sword, keeping her eyes locked with those of the man she once loved. Cradling the pommel with her palm, Helena laughed. 'This isn't fear. This is rage.'

Helena shoved her sword further into his body with all her might, pushing him off and away from her. Her body twitched as pain swept through her, holding her captive upon the gravel. She squeezed her eyes shut and fought back whimpers.

'Helena!'

Catherine slid across the ground, skidding to Helena's side. She let go of her sword and pulled her head onto her lap, running her hand across her undead cheek. Though she knew

A Knight's Blood

Helena would heal rather quickly, seeing the blood pool underneath her sent panic hurdling through her thoughts. Her own chest ached to see Helena so vulnerable. In that moment, all she saw was a re-enactment of the night Erik took Walter from her. Tears welled as she struggled to keep her breaths from catching in her throat.

Erik struggled to get back onto his feet with a groan. His axe clattered to the ground near his feet as he grasped the hilt of Helena's sword. Pulling the longsword from his stomach made him wretch, but he continued despite that. A gasp fell from his lips as he finally freed the sword from his body. He dropped it, stepping away as it clanged hitting the ground.

The noise pulled Helena's attention away from Catherine's glassy eyes. She watched Erik stumble and pick up his axe. She turned back to Catherine, trying to remain calm while she moved her head off the knight's lap. 'Run.'

She followed Helena's gaze and saw Erik coming towards them. Catherine reached for her sword but was just too slow.

Erik swung his axe at her and slashed Catherine's right arm, cutting her forearm before she could even touch her weapon.

Catherine yelped. She brought her shield up in front of her, catching his chin on its edge. She fell back, scrambling to put some distance between Erik and herself. Her arm weakened the more weight she put on it. The wound stung as blood wept steadily, soaking her sleeve and staining it red.

No matter how much pain she was in, Helena couldn't let Erik get close to Catherine. She crawled towards Erik's feet and grabbed his ankle. Helena wrapped her hand over the other, scrunched her face and yanked with all her might.

He lifted his other foot off the ground and fell flat on his face. Erik turned to glare at Helena, ignoring the fact that Catherine ran past and picked up her sword. He kicked back at the other vampire, hitting her in the face. Gravel crunched under his boots as he jumped back onto his feet.

Helena groaned as her head pounded. Her hands fell away from his ankle. Her body tried to knit itself back together so fast that it sent her vision into a tailspin. Pain overwhelmed her senses and forced her eyes closed. Her hands went limp and her head flopped to the gravel below.

Catherine saw Helena lying on the ground and stopped. Tears returned to her eyes as memories of Walter dead flashed in her mind. Both anger and sorrow grasped Catherine's thoughts and refused to let go. She came back to her senses when Erik pulled her sword out of her hand and threw it into the chapel's debris.

He swung his axe at her head, snarling as it hit her shield. His axe collided with her shield again with an almighty clank. Erik tried to pull his axe back, but grimaced when it remained lodged in Catherine's shield.

Upon realising his error, Catherine tossed her shield across the courtyard. She watched the moonlight illuminate the metal as it spun through the air. Upon noticing that Erik was watching his axe and her shield fly away from them, she sprinted for her sword.

Erik saw her run from out of the corner of his eye and quickly caught up to her, tackling her to the chapel tiles and landing with a loud crack.

The tile underneath Catherine split upon impact. All breath was stolen from her body. Pain radiated across her back, forcing her to take shallow and rapid gasps. Tears blurred her vision, distorting Erik's face as he loomed over her. She ran her trembling hand across her belt, feeling for her dagger.

He wrapped his hand around Catherine's throat, pulling away when her necklace singed his flesh. Erik clutched his hand and glanced at the scorched line across his palm, watching the area darkened to grey and spread down his wrist and up his fingers. He grimaced, his hand shaking from the radiant burn.

Despite the pain from touching silver, he grasped the chain with his wounded hand, crying out as he yanked it from Catherine's neck. A link in the chain snapped and he threw it as far away from him as possible. His red irises stared down at the knight, narrowing as he watched her struggle to catch her breath.

Sweat beaded upon Catherine's forehead. She licked her lips to moisten them and help her lungs draw in air. The dagger's pommel chilled her fingertips as she brushed past it, reminding her of where it rested. Catherine grasped the hilt, her knuckles turning white. She clenched her free hand into a fist and swung at Erik, knowing full well he'd catch it before it connected.

All she needed was a distraction.

Erik caught her hand and slammed her arm against the ground, holding it up above her head. He smirked down at her, flashing his fangs. One side of his face appeared hollow and was blotched with both bruises and blood, the remainder of Helena's earlier punch. His nails dug into her wrist, drawing blood where he came into contact with her skin. Delight danced in the darkness of his pupils.

'I don't know how you got to know her or see through our glamour, but you should've chosen your allies more wisely, Lady Seymour,' he said, sneering. 'You could've avoided dying.'

She glared up at Erik, keeping his gaze on hers as she

slipped her dagger out of its sheath. The blade snugly laid against her thigh. Catherine aggressively snorted and shook her head at him.

'No,' she replied. 'I made the right choice. You, however, made the wrong one.'

Before his smug smirk even left his lips, Catherine raised the dagger high and plunged it into his chest. She yanked the blade from his body and stabbed him again and again, clenching her teeth to put as much strength behind her strikes as she could manage.

Erik shrieked as the sharp silver charred the flesh around it. His skin and the muscle underneath bubbled and turned grey, corrupting the veins connected to it. He tightened his grip on her wrist with every strike, cutting off the blood flow to her hand and threatening to snap bones. Wincing and hissing, he caught her forearm and pinned it to the ground above her head like the other. His chest spasmed as he stared right at the bloodied blade still in her hand.

The knight's eyes widened. Panic coursed through her thoughts and took hold of her racing heart. She fought to free her arms from his grasp, turning her wrist as much as she could to try and stick Erik with her dagger again.

Helena's words echoed in her head, sending shivers down her spine. Blood gave their magic enough power to heal wounds made from silver. And Erik could easily bite her and drain her dry.

She kicked and screamed. The knight wriggled her head and torso back and forth, trying her very hardest not to get bitten while she was trapped. Catherine launched the top of her head up at Erik's, slamming into his nose and breaking the cartilage upon impact.

Erik did not let go. He didn't loosen his grip or even shift his weight off her stomach.

Catherine squeezed her eyes shut and moved her neck as far away from his snapping jaws as she could. Her wrist twinged as she twisted it as best as she could, swinging the tip of her dagger as close to him as her limited range could get. Dread settled in her chest, constricting her ribs. Her glassy eyes darted left and right, hoping, praying, that Helena was able to get to her feet once more.

Much to her dismay, Erik's fangs found purchase. She gasped as he bit down on her neck, sending burning pain shooting through her jaw and shoulder.

He removed his teeth from her neck, only to bite her harder the second time. Erik's grip on her arms loosened. He hungrily siphoned the blood from her body, humming as his wounds started to heal. The first to knit together were those that weren't inflicted with silver.

Tears slid down her cheeks. She folded her lips between her teeth to mitigate the pain. Catherine stared up at the sky, watching the stars begin to spin above her. The ground underneath her wavered. Fatigue settled in her bones, weighing her limbs down. One by one, the stars were extinguished. No matter how hard she fought, the darkness behind the stars threatened to swallow her whole.

Catherine yelped as Erik's mouth was forced off her neck. Her chest shuddered, trying to catch her breath once more now that she had some freedom of movement. Her tear-streaked vision reflected multiples of the copper-haired vampire and her blazing crimson eyes. The wounds on Helena's chest had stopped bleeding but were far from properly healed.

Helena stood over her, her expression furious and fearsome. She held Erik's head away from Catherine by a fistful of blond braids. Helena ripped him away the knight, dragging him onto the gravel outside the chapel ruins. She threw him to the ground, dropping to her knees and pinning him against the ground with a snarl.

Erik's face, despite the fact his broken bones had almost fully healed, was covered in Catherine's blood. His eyes were glazed over with hunger. He thrashed about on the ground, swinging his fists around with a strangled yell.

Anger seethed through Helena as she glared down at the vampire she despised.

Helena tightened her grip on his hair, wrapping his braids around her knuckles. She set her other hand on his chin and twisted.

A sickening crack echoed.

Helena didn't stop. She tore his head from his neck, letting his body flop to the ground. Erik's head hung from her hand, trailing blood as it swung.

Bloodlust and pain were tangled together in a dangerous dance, colouring Helena's thoughts red. Her anger subsided upon realising she had finally destroyed her nemesis.

The knight could barely keep her eyes open. Relief flooded her thoughts. Her heart beat slower and slower as blood seeped from her body. She forced herself to turn onto her side, watching as Helena glanced down at the head still in her hand.

The copper-haired vampire turned to check on Catherine,

dropping Erik's head as their gaze met.

She rushed to Catherine's side, collapsing to her knees next to her. Helena pulled her as gently as possible onto her lap. Her fingers brushed Catherine's cheek over and over, hoping the soft tingles that followed soothed the knight's racing mind.

Catherine fought back against sleep's irresistible lure.

'It's okay. He's dead,' Helena whispered. 'Stay with me.'

Catherine clenched her dagger tighter, trying to ground herself with its weight.

She held the knight tenderly. Helena closed her eyes for a moment, trying to ignore the blood on Catherine's neck.

The smell was utterly intoxicating, how could she not want to drink a little?

She leant down and lapped the blood that pooled on Catherine's neck. She just needed enough to have the deep gashes on her chest scab over and so she could take the knight up to the manor as fast as her undead abilities would allow.

Helena sighed as soon as it touched her tongue.

Her wounds began to knit themselves back together as she continued to drink.

Catherine's eyes slid closed. The tension in her body loosened so much that she became nothing more than a ragdoll. Her consciousness began to slip into a state similar to that deep sleep.

This was just how she pictured it: dying to protect her people.

Her fingers relaxed, letting the dagger fall from her palm.

The clang of the dagger hitting tile shook Helena from her daze. She forced herself to move away from the knight's neck so she wouldn't continue drinking Catherine's blood.

The vampire lifted Catherine up from the ground, cradling her against her healed chest. She looked down at her peaceful expression, fighting back the panic that bubbled in the back of her throat. She sprinted for the manor, holding Catherine close. Her weakening heartbeat thumped against Helena's arm, kindling the hope that Catherine's eyes would open once more.

21

She didn't remember how she got there, but Catherine awoke in her bed. Heavy velvet curtains covered the windows, keeping Catherine ignorant of the current time of day. The hearth blazed with orange flames, warming the room with its soft glow. Though she was thoroughly bundled up in her bed and covered in blankets, said warmth didn't make a difference. Shivers continued to dance upon her flesh.

A foul odour crept towards her nostrils. Her face instinctively contorted in disgust. Bandages covered in strong-smelling herbs were wrapped around her wounds, putting pressure on the area to stem any bleeding should they reopen.

Catherine groaned and attempted to sit up. She propped herself up on her elbows and winced as the room span around her.

'She's awake!' Helena exclaimed.

Aldric jumped up from the stool beside Catherine's bed, both panicked and relieved to see she was awake and wanting to move. He helped her sit back against the nest of pillows without injuring herself further. Prolonged worry gave him deep wrinkles under his eyes, exaggerating his already dark circles.

'Take it easy, you've lost a lot of blood,' Aldric explained.

The last thing she remembered was being in the

vampire's arms and seeing fear wrack her beautiful face as darkness swallowed her whole. Catherine looked around the room, hoping to see Helena, but the copper-haired vampire was nowhere in sight. She could've sworn she'd heard her only a moment before.

'Cat, you've been asleep for a few days,' Aldric said. 'We were worried you wouldn't wake up at all.'

He placed his hands on his knees and drew in a breath, his body shaking as he inhaled. The whites of Aldric's eyes were red and glassy. A tear slid down his cheek as he smiled at Catherine, relief lightening his previously grim expression.

Catherine's chest tightened at the sight of Aldric's sorrow. Guilt twisted in her gut. She pressed her lips together, trying her hardest not to cry along with him.

'Helena told me what happened,' Aldric continued. He played with his fingers, keeping his mind occupied on that instead of the emotions racing through his thoughts. 'Thank you for dispatching Erik with Helena. The people can rest easy knowing that their biggest threat is no more. You had us worried, but I'm glad you're awake.'

'Thank you,' Catherine whispered. She mustered the courage to look at Aldric, weakly smiling at him. 'She was right about him being dangerous. He needed to be put down. Erik was considering making Birkstead a blood farm for him and his new coven.'

He gently placed his hand on her shoulder, returning her smile. 'Your father may not say it, but I will. I'm proud of you. Walter would be too.'

Tears welled in the corners of her eyes. She let herself cry alongside Aldric. Happiness and sorrow mingled in her chest, replaying those last two phrases over and over.

'Thanks,' Catherine replied. 'Although I appreciate it, I can't take all the credit. Helena was right, a single knight wouldn't be able to kill powerful vampires like him without assistance from other knights or even supernatural beings like other vampires.'

'I told you so,' Helena called from her hiding place.

Catherine turned to find the vampire, wincing when a wound on her neck reopened. The wound's edge itched when the scab pulled away from her skin.

'I told you to take it easy,' Aldric chastised. 'You're not going to heal at all if you keep reopening your wounds.'

He helped Catherine settle her head back down against her pillows. A frown pinched his brows when he removed the bandage and saw spots of blood dotting the poultice that had been slathered over it. He shook his head with a disappointed hum as he reached for the washbasin of water. The bandage fell to the floor with a wet squelch. He wrung the water out of a clean rag.

She smiled, letting out a strangled snort. Catherine had seen him act similarly caring for his daughter after she fell and scraped her knee a few months prior. Her heart warmed as she realised that he was treating her as if she was his own.

He dabbed the rag against her neck, carefully cleaning the area. Aldric understood that she was determined to prove herself and protect her people, but he wasn't pleased with her recklessness.

'Helena, please show yourself. I'm only going to upset

Aldric if I look for you.'

Aldric playfully slapped her arm with the rag, smiling as Catherine chuckled.

The wardrobe door creaked open, revealing a pair of crimson eyes staring at Catherine. Nothing else about the vampire was visible in the wardrobe's darkness, but Catherine could just tell there was a grin upon her lips.

The vampire stepped out from the wardrobe and let the door swing shut behind her.

Catherine was right. There indeed was a grin upon Helena's lips.

Firelight danced upon her copper hair, making it appear as if it were metal just pulled from a forge. Helena crossed the room and sat down on the bed beside Catherine's legs.

'Good to see you're all healed,' Catherine said, envious of the vampire's miraculous healing ability.

Aldric redressed Catherine's neck with a clean bandage.

'Our weapons are under your bed. Aldric retrieved them before they could be picked up by a curious villager. Erik's fangs were harvested and his body has been reduced to ashes. Your father wants his remains sent to the Church, so I kept them at the bottom of your wardrobe so you can present them yourself,' Helena explained. 'I won't let him belittle your victory. You deserve the chance to gloat.'

'Thank you,' Catherine breathed.

'You're welcome,' Helena said. 'That vile vampire

needed to be put down anyhow. I'm glad that you were there beside me to do so.'

Catherine's mind wandered. She stared at the fireplace, letting her thoughts trample through her mind. Feeling slowly returned to her hands she reached for the cross that usually hung around her neck. She grasped the top of her shift and froze as realisation settled in.

Her mother's necklace was missing.

Erik had ripped it from her neck and thrown it into Birkstead.

'What's wrong?' Helena asked.

Unfamiliar emptiness filled Catherine's chest. She stroked her skin, feeling for the pendant that wasn't there.

'My mother's necklace...' Catherine replied, her voice breaking. Despair flooded her mind and body.

Helena saw Catherine's hand sitting upon her sternum and realised what she was talking about. The vampire's shoulders drooped as she turned her attention to the tears trembling upon the knight's lashes.

'Oh Catherine,' she said, rising to her feet. 'I can go look for i-'

Before Helena could finish speaking, Catherine shook her head.

'Please don't look for it right now,' Catherine replied. 'Especially if it's still daylight. I'd rather have company than the necklace at the moment. If it can't be found, hopefully there's something still hidden away in mother's study for me to find.

231

There are still so many unanswered questions I wish I could ask her.'

Helena sat back down on Catherine's bed, patting her knee. 'You don't have to pretend that losing your mother's necklace doesn't bother you. Aldric knows how much it means to you and I'd be devastated if I misplaced my father's sword.'

Aldric turned to Helena, his brow raised in confusion. 'You'd really be devastated? I thought you hated your father?'

'Sure, I despise the man, but it's all I have left of my life before I reawakened. I doubt anything else from that time in my life remains.'

Catherine closed her eyes and drew in a shaky breath. She laid back down against her pillows, sinking into them as if they were made of soft sand. Her pulse pounded against her ears, slowing gradually as her initial panic passed.

Aldric picked up the basin and the old bandage and rose to his feet.

'I'm going to get some more ointment from the healers. You two behave while I'm gone,' he announced, turning his gaze to Helena, cocking his head to the side in warning.

Helena rolled her eyes and chuckled. 'Don't worry, we will.'

With that, Aldric left the room and closed the door behind him.

Crackles and pops from the logs in the fireplace disrupted the growing tension, but didn't destroy it. Nothing was said. Nothing needed to be said. The way in which they looked at each other awakened a deeper longing for the other's touch.

A Knight's Blood

Helena sighed and pulled her hand away from the knight's knee when she could no longer hear Aldric's footsteps in the hallway.

Catherine shuffled back against the pillows to sit up a little bit more. Her body ached every centimetre she moved, but felt it was worth it when she was comfortable and could see the vampire's beautiful face better. Warmth crept onto her cheeks, colouring them pink when she caught Helena's gaze.

Guilt wracked Helena's thoughts. She turned away from Catherine for a moment. No matter how much she wanted to, touching her would only aggravate her wounds further. Helena shifted closer, refusing to touch any patch of skin close to the bandages wrapped around her bruised flesh.

'It wasn't my intention for you to get hurt as badly as you are,' Helena said. 'I knew that injury was inevitable, we were fighting a powerful vampire after all, but I didn't think there was a risk of you potentially dying. I thought that I'd be able to protect you.'

'The thought of you intentionally letting me get so injured I could die hadn't crossed my mind,' Catherine admitted. 'Not then. Not now. If we had teamed up the night you and Erik first fought in Birkstead, I would've thought you wouldn't have cared if I lived or not simply because you were a vampire. I now know that's not the truth.'

'You might not be as lethargic as you are now if things hadn't happened the way they did. I drank your blood without asking. In the moment, I thought there was no other way I could get you here fast enough to save your life. While the cavity in my chest wasn't fully healed, it gave me enough strength to get you to the manor as quick as I could,' Helena said.

Catherine smiled weakly. 'You weren't the one to bite

me in the first place. If you hadn't had any blood, I'd likely be dead. Though, I am a little curious as to why you didn't try to reawaken me if you were so concerned about me dying.'

'As I've told you before, it's a very distressing process, even if you agree to it knowing what to expect. I want it to be a decision you make. I didn't want to take that choice from you,' Helena explained, clasping Catherine's hand and holding it tight.

Catherine couldn't help but to let her smile widen. Though it hurt to move, she stroked Helena's impeccably soft cheek. She ran her thumb across Helena's cheekbones, embracing how her heart fluttered when the vampire leant into her touch.

'I appreciate your thoughtfulness,' Catherine replied. She winced as her bicep trembled trying to hold up the weight of her own arm. 'Thank you, Helena.'

Helena opened her mouth to speak, but couldn't find the words she wanted to say. Her crimson gaze remained firmly fixated on how utterly spellbinding Catherine's genuine smile was. She shifted closer, sitting beside the knight's torso. The vampire brushed wisps of Catherine's dark hair away from her eyes, her fingertips ghosting the knight's forehead. She tightened her hand around Catherine's, revelling in her strong pulse thumping underneath her skin.

Catherine tried her hardest to keep her breaths even but that failed to calm her nerves. Butterflies thrashed around in Catherine's stomach as relief graced Helena's pretty face. Never before had she felt so seen and understood by someone before, let alone someone who stirred up her insides every time she smiled. She continued to stroke the vampire's cheek, embracing the excitement warming her chest. Thankfully, she was so enamoured with Helena that ignoring the painful twinges in her arm came as easily as breathing.

Helena brushed Catherine's face with her fingertips, tracing the knight's jawline. She rested her forefinger under Catherine's chin and grinned down at her. 'I have a feeling I know what you're thinking.'

'Is that so?'

Helena chuckled at the mischievous quirk of Catherine's brow. 'Shall we see if I'm right?'

Unable to articulate her anticipation and curiosity with words, Catherine nodded.

Helena closed her eyes and leant in close, bringing her lips to Catherine's. Her finger circled the soft skin underneath the knight's chin as soon as she felt Catherine's warm lips touched her own.

She leant into Helena's kiss, ignoring the twinges in her neck while struggling to get closer to the vampire. The lack of heartbeat chilling Helena's touch sent shivers down the knight's spine. Catherine wanted more of her. No, she *needed* more.

A smile tugged at the corners of Helena's lips. There was no sound sweeter than the small moans vibrating upon Catherine's lips. She drew back, smiling wider when Catherine whined at the loss of her touch. Helena chuckled and returned her lips to Catherine's again, just as eager to feel close to Catherine as Catherine did Helena.

Before either had the chance to deepen the kiss, the door creaked open.

Helena pulled away from Catherine and slid across the bed to appear as if they hadn't been kissing. She smiled innocently at Aldric.

The older knight looked at Catherine and Helena, snorting with amusement as he closed the door with his foot. He knew the vampire enough to recognise that her innocent smile was usually masking something she'd done. A basket swung from the crook of his elbow and settled against his hip when he stopped moving. His gaze settled on that of the injured, and now embarrassed, knight in her bed.

Catherine stared back at Aldric, her face red and her eyes wide.

Aldric set the basket full of goodies down on the floor beside her bed. 'It seems I've interrupted something.'

'Perhaps,' Helena answered. A mischievous smirk graced her lips. 'Why? Did you wish to join us?'

Aldric chuckled. 'Thank you for the offer, but I'm spoken for.'

'Your loss,' Helena replied, shrugging.

Both Aldric and Helena laughed at the joke.

Catherine, however, glanced between the two of them in horror. Pain be damned, she wanted to yank the covers over her head and hope the ground would swallow both her and her bed whole.

'Don't worry,' Aldric said, his voice tender. 'Your secret is safe with me.'

Though she remained on edge, Catherine relaxed against her pillows.

A Knight's Blood

The vampire tucked a few dark stray hairs behind Catherine's ear and ran her thumb across her cheek.

'Does anyone else know I'm awake?' Catherine asked.

'As far as I'm aware, the only person who knows is Sabina. She insisted I bring you a sachet of dried lavender to help you sleep and some fresh tourtelets in fryture to help keep your spirits up,' Aldric replied.

'Thank you,' Catherine said, closing her eyes and humming with delight. 'And please give my thanks to Sabina. She knows those are my favourite.'

'You're welcome.' Aldric's gentle smile fell when he turned towards Helena. 'And you might want to find some other way to keep yourself occupied for the time being; Cat needs rest.'

The vampire pouted and crossed her arms, opening her mouth to protest.

Aldric tilted his head downward, crossing his arms and staring at her with the same intensity when he was dealing his own sulking daughter. 'Helena, out.'

'Fine,' Helena said, groaning.

The vampire got up from the knight's bed. She bent down and pressed a kiss upon Catherine's head before she left the room.

Catherine smiled up at her, watching her with a wistful sigh.

Aldric placed the basket on the table beside her. He too left the room, closing the door behind him again.

Silence swept through the room the moment Aldric left. A slight breeze from the door closing drifted towards the fireplace, forcing the flames to wriggle and writhe against its confines.

Catherine went to reach for the phantom of her mother's necklace, clutching her shift's collar with as much strength as she could muster.

She reached over to the basket and picked up one of the tourteletes, biting into it. Catherine savoured how the honey stuck to her tongue and balanced out the figs nestled within the pastry. As delicious as they were, eating the one sapped what little energy she had left. Fatigue set in quicker than she expected.

She tried to clear her mind to eventually nap, but her memories insisted on replaying the sensation of Helena's lips on hers.

22

Much to Catherine's disappointment, her father found out that she was awake sooner than she wanted. She wished her covers could hide her from the world, but she knew that would never work anywhere outside the confines of her fantasies.

She was certain that Geoffrey wanted to hear she failed and use the moment to belittle her. She was also certain that he wouldn't accept the fact she had indeed completed his task. He never told her Walter didn't count towards the two sets of remains she needed, so Erik's remains were the final set.

Sabina sat on Catherine's bed, holding her hand as if she were comforting her own child during a bout of illness. The noblewoman smiled sadly and placed the bag containing Erik's remains on Catherine's lap.

'Thank you,' the knight said. 'I don't think I could get out of bed without injuring myself further.'

'You're welcome. Your father will wish to speak to you sooner rather than later. It would be beneficial for you to have the one thing that would give you power before he arrives.'

Catherine swallowed what little saliva coated her tongue. Her free hand clasped the bag's ties, holding it close to her stomach. Her brows pinched together as she stared down at the pouch, lamenting on how Erik's ashes and fangs would allow her to have some say in her future. And yet, she couldn't shake the feeling that completing the quest wouldn't change a thing.

'What's on your mind?' Sabina asked.

There was no use hiding from Sabina. The noblewoman was as sharp as she was compassionate.

Catherine sighed. 'I fear that he will not honour his word. No matter how hard I try, he'll always push for me to do as he wants, even if he has to break promises to do so.'

'I know you're already feeling a little defeated, but you have more power than you realise. Lord Seymour will have a hard time disputing you if you already have the upper hand,' Sabina explained, nodding to the remains. 'You've worked too hard to give up now.'

Catherine looked at the bag of ash, imagining a proud smile on her father's face. That image soon disintegrated when she realised that could only happen in her wildest dreams. Her father never showed her affection before, why would he now?

She reached for the neckline of her shift, grabbing for the cross that was no longer there.

Without announcing himself or even greeting Catherine, Geoffrey walked in through the door and stopped at the foot of his daughter's bed.

'I'll wait for him to leave and come back in. Good luck,' Sabina whispered, squeezing her hand and holding it tight.

Sabina got up and closed the door behind her, leaving the two of them alone.

Though a fire raged in the hearth behind Geoffrey, an icy chill descended upon the room. It wasn't the familiar chill of silver alerting to the presence of undead, but the familiar chill between father and daughter.

A Knight's Blood

Geoffrey frowned at Catherine. He crossed his arms, glaring down at her with disdain.

'Ah, so she lives,' he sneered.

'That I do,' Catherine replied. She patted the bag containing Erik's remains and held it out for her father to take. 'Another set of vampiric remains for the Church. It is the reason by I have been out of action and why your new friend, Erik, will no longer visit.'

'And why is that?' Geoffrey asked, glossing over the implication of her words.

'Erik was the vampire who killed and reawakened Sir Alwyn. He was charming you to turn Birkstead into his own personal blood farm,' Catherine snapped. 'You're welcome, by the way.'

Annoyance tugged Geoffrey's features downwards, appearing to age him dramatically. It was clear he didn't expect her to complete the quest he'd given her.

'Well, I should commend you on your tenacity to see a quest to its end. I assumed you'd give up or kill yourself trying,' Geoffrey announced, snatching the pouch from Catherine's hand.

The knight narrowed her eyes at her father, clenching her hands into fists. 'Maybe if that happened, you would finally go and find yourself another wife to have a son with. That way, you wouldn't have to go to such lengths marrying off the daughter you don't seem to care for.'

He narrowed his eyes at her. 'Your accomplishments and cynical comments won't change the fact that I've found a suitable match for you. A French nobleman looking to join the English court. You will be able to visit the French court, explore a new country, learn a new language… There will be very little for you to complain about because you'll be so busy helping him fit in with our circle as he will be with you.'

Catherine's stomach sank. A wave of nausea swept through her.

It was just as she thought. Whether she had completed the task he set her or not, Geoffrey was only interested in serving his own interests.

Nausea made way for the rage she usually kept reigned in. Catherine's hands shook, her knuckles turning white as her fists tightened. Her heart thumped against her ribs. If it didn't hurt to move or even breathe, she'd pounce on him and beat his face to a bloody pulp.

'You are perfectly content to treat me as if I'm a jewel to sell to the highest bidder. I, however, will lose everything I worked to achieve. This nobleman you're marrying me off to will likely expect me to become nothing more than a possession designed to birth his babies. You are perfectly aware of this. You married mother, and made her nothing more than a thing that carried your heir. The work she did for the Church only served to elevate your position while you did the bare minimum.'

'That was not my choice. God and the Church are the ones who insist that a woman must obey her husband. The rest of us are simply following the example set by those who wish to see us join our Lord in Heaven,' Geoffrey replied. 'Your mother went above and beyond what was expected of her, even if there were aspects of those expectations she disagreed with. You'd be wise to follow her example.'

Anger and sorrow grasped her heart and mind, refusing

to let logic find any footing in the flood of thoughts cluttering her skull. Nothing he did or said frightened her anymore; he was already about to strip away everything she fought tooth and nail to keep whether she'd succeeded or not. She had no sword, but this had to be her final stand against his scheme to control the rest of her life. He had no qualms about hitting her where it hurt, why should she have any qualms about hurting him?

'Then you admit mother's death occurred because you forced her to go along with what God and His Church asked of you?' Catherine asked bluntly. 'And now you wish to doom your only child to that same fate without a second thought. The amount of money you paid the Church in Indulgences may buy you a place in Heaven, but it does not protect you from His judgement. It also doesn't protect me from paying the price for your choices. We know that God would not think twice to punish a son for his father's transgressions; He would punish a daughter for the same just as quickly.'

Geoffrey's face went beet red. He rounded the corner of her bed to stand beside her, his boots thumping against the floor like thunder. 'I ought to have your tongue removed for the venom you spit!'

'Why? Because I speak the truth?' she asked, her voice low and her gaze dangerous. 'You don't have to keep the truth from me anymore. I know the Church killed mother. And like the coward you are, you did nothing to stop them.'

Geoffrey's eyes widened. He couldn't believe what she'd just said. He took a step back, staring at her in shock. A few seconds after the initial surprise faded, he breathed in through his nose, puffing his chest out to try and intimidate his wounded daughter.

'I don't know how you found out, but you shouldn't

speak on matters you know nothing about. I couldn't stop them from killing her, but Agnes knew I could stop them from doing the same to you. She begged me not to let them hurt you. I saved you because she asked me to. You owe me your life.'

Catherine narrowed her eyes at Geoffrey. Her hands trembled as she folded her fingers into her palms, wishing that she could be clutching her sword or even her dagger instead of the air. Even if what he said was true, she'd just about had enough of his theatrics.

'I owe you nothing! I ought to drag you into Birkstead by the scruff of your thinning hair and rip your head from your body. You claim I am the one who shames you with my actions, but you shame yourself without any help from me.'

Geoffrey grabbed her by the throat. His hand threatened to squeeze tighter should she dare speak again.

'You don't get to threaten me, Catherine. If it weren't for this arrangement, you wouldn't inherit the manor, let alone your beloved village,' Geoffrey exclaimed, spittle raining down upon her face. 'You are only worth as much as who you marry. You'll be third cousin-in-law to the Dauphiné once you've married this man. Our family will be elevated thanks to me and the children you will bear.'

In the past, she would've begrudgingly held her tongue. But now, she was never going to give him the satisfaction of seeing fear on her face ever again. Wrath continued to bubble within her chest, threatening to consume her.

Despite the pain that came from lifting her arms earlier, Catherine unclenched her fists and dug her nails into his wrist, drawing blood. The knight bared her clenched teeth and pried his fingers from her throat with her other hand, bending them as far

244

back as she could without a care if she broke bones or not.

Her father cried out and drew his hand away, cradling it with his other hand. Tears of pain welled in his eyes. Geoffrey stared at his daughter, fear blooming on his face.

Catherine glared at him from underneath her brows. She rested her hands upon her lap, placing the one with his blood underneath her fingernails on top. Though she finally embraced the anger she'd partially repressed, seeing her father so scared of her sent sickly-sweet thrills sprinting through her mind. Oh, how she wished she had Helena's fangs. The knight tilted her head to the side, refusing to break eye contact with Geoffrey.

'I do not need a man to tell me my worth. I don't even need God Himself to tell me my worth. That is determined by me and me alone. You misunderstand me when I tell you I do not need a husband. A husband would only get in my way. He'd claim my ideas and actions as his own. I would only serve his desire to boost his ego and further his bloodline. I would be nothing but a prop and I despise being thought of as property. Do not even think for a moment that some man will be able to control me. He can try, but I won't guarantee that he would survive. I have fought multiple vampires and lived to see another sunrise. Some of the best knights in England cannot say the same. Saving me from death as a child doesn't mean you're entitled to orchestrating my future without consulting me.'

Before Geoffrey could get a word in, Catherine continued to berate him.

'Though the noblemen you call friends applaud your efforts to line your pockets, you forget the role you're meant to perform as Lord of Birkstead. You extort and threaten the very people you've been entrusted to protect. Cutting costs at the expense of Birkstead's wellbeing may impress your friends, but those people deserve better. If you think that someone cannot match up to you, you treat them like pawns in your games. I hope those Indulgences you paid for were worth it. Not even God can save you from yourself,' Catherine finished, her words dripping with a venom her father had never heard from her before.

Geoffrey's jaw dropped.

Catherine smirked with a smugness she wouldn't have dared shown in front of him before. She had often thought of how satisfying it would be to leave her father speechless. The rush and satisfaction from doing so was even more intense than she expected, quickly finding herself addicted to the feeling.

'I realise that you are upset with me for orchestrating this match, but you are not in a position to dispute your responsibilities as a noblewoman and my only child. It doesn't matter what you say, you will marry who I say and that is that,' Geoffrey declared.

Her glee waned and her rage returned. Catherine's expression darkened at her father's words. She opened her mouth to argue back.

Geoffrey raised his hand to silence her.

'Catherine,' Geoffrey warned. 'No matter how much you argue with me, it won't change my mind or delay the plans I've set in motion. You will do as you are told.'

Once he finished speaking, he lowered his hand and watched his daughter carefully.

'I see,' Catherine replied. 'My future has already been

decided for me. You didn't even check if I had succumbed to my wounds before you arranged this match, did you?'

'Catherine...'

The knight shook her head, ignoring the pain shooting up the sides of her neck. 'Then I have no choice but to accept my fate,' she resigned.

Geoffrey folded his arms across his chest and watched his daughter with uncertainty. 'Are you being truthful?' Geoffrey questioned. 'I do not have time or patience to deal with your antics.'

'Provided I am allowed time to heal from my wounds, I will marry this Frenchman you have chosen for me,' Catherine announced, furrowing her brows and clenching her fists again.

Relief flooded his face. Geoffrey placed his hand on his daughter's bruised shoulder, smiling down at her as if praising a child for completing a simple task they previously struggled with.

Finally, she received that smile she'd been waiting for. And yet, it felt incredibly hollow. A smile birthed from a false admission of defeat was not the way in which she wanted to receive the loving smile she'd longed for from her father.

'Thank you, Catherine. I'm glad you have finally decided to become the woman you were born to be. You will be allowed time to heal. I shall let you rest. We will discuss the details when you feel better.'

He patted her shoulder and ignored the way in which she flinched in pain.

Her expression remained unchanged. She remained

wrathful even as tears welled in the corner of her eyes. 'However...'

Geoffrey's smile faded. He snatched his hand away from her shoulder, staring at her as if he'd just touched the flames in the fireplace on the other side of the room.

'I will make the whole ordeal Hell for both of you. By the time the wedding takes place, you will wish that vampires had killed me. The Church may even decide I'm still as much of a risk as mother was and kill me like they did her. If you force me to marry, whatever life you have left to live will not be lived in peace. You will suffer until your last breath. I will personally ensure it.'

Geoffrey sighed. 'Very well. Do your worst.'

He left her bedroom without another word.

Tears of frustration spilled down her cheeks as soon as the door closed. Pain coursed through her entire body, trapping her in its unyielding grasp. Her lungs burned. Catherine scrunched her eyes closed and slammed her fists against her bed.

No matter how much she wished the ground would swallow her whole, she wanted Helena by her side. The vampire would know what to say and do to ease her distress.

The door opened again.

Relief flooded through her as Sabina poked her head in through the doorway.

Sabina slipped into the room and closed the door as quietly as possible. She dropped her hands down by her side as she crossed the room and sat back down on Catherine's bed. Her hand grasped Catherine's clean one, squeezing it reassuringly tight.

'Are you alright?' Sabina asked, knowing the answer before it was spoken.

Wisps of dark hair fell upon Catherine's forehead as she shook her head, trying to stop crying.

'No. He's going to marry me to some nobleman from France despite the fact I completed the task. Everything I did was for nothing.'

The noblewoman carefully pulled Catherine into a hug, gently rubbing her back as the knight tried not to cry. Sabina rested her head on top of Catherine's. Her gaze remained fixed on the door, her ire for Geoffrey threatening to burn a pair of holes through the wood.

'It wasn't for nothing,' Sabina whispered. 'You've proven that you're capable of more than your father thought. My husband tells me that your peers respect you more than ever before, isn't that worth something?'

'How far can respect get when father holds something over almost every knight in the surrounding area?' Catherine asked, sniffing back her tears. 'He holds your daughter's education over Aldric. I'm sure Robert's training and equipment is being funded by my father too. I wouldn't expect any of them to give that up simply because they respect me.'

Sabina's gentle hands smoothed Catherine's dark hair, stroking the back of her head and neck. 'It might make your time as Lady Birkstead easier if you command the respect of the others.'

Though Catherine doubted that would be the case, she

couldn't help but to reminisce about how Sabina's touch felt so similar to that of her mother's. Her tears continued to fall even as she tried to stop them.

Memories of her mother's loving gestures and sweet smile flooded her thoughts. The knight couldn't help but to wonder what life would have been like if the Church hadn't killed Agnes, her mother. There had to be a reason why her employers decided they couldn't allow her to live and why they almost did the same to her daughter. What about her mother's research into vampires that was so dangerous and damning she had to die for it?

Her tears dried as she thought of her mother's abandoned study and the potential secrets that remained waiting for her to find. If Agnes had truly pitched the idea of hiring vampires to protect peasants from other vampires to the Church, what else had she uncovered that Catherine still had yet to learn? How many vampires had she spoken with to come to that conclusion? Catherine's blooming relationship with Helena had opened her eyes to the fact some members of the undead hunted their own for amusement and profit, how many more like her existed and were willing to speak to Agnes? How much more could Catherine learn about protecting people from vampires if she became one herself?

'You know, being married isn't a death sentence,' Sabina said, still stroking the back of Catherine's head.

The woman's voice pulled Catherine out of her thoughts and back into reality.

'Luck might be on your side and you end up with someone who is kind and understanding,' she continued. 'They might even appreciate your training and let you continue your knightly duties.'

Despite the fact that moving forced a grimace to her face, Catherine sat back against her pillows to stare at Sabina with shock. Her glassy, irritated eyes teared up again. She shook her head slightly. Betrayal slithered down her spine and prickled her arms with goosebumps.

'I don't care if this Frenchman is the kindest person in the world, I will not marry him. My father could find the next son of God and I still wouldn't marry him,' Catherine replied, her voice laced with the same venom she used on Geoffrey before. 'There will never be a day where I will marry a man and give Birkstead to someone who won't care about the people living there. Why would I doom myself to listening to someone I could never love, let alone find attractive?'

Sabina sighed and patted the knight's hand. 'Catherine-'

'No, you don't understand.' She snatched her hand away, whimpering as the quick movement aggravated her bruises and aching muscles.

'Then help me understand,' Sabina pleaded. 'Aldric and I can't help you if you don't tell us what's going on.'

Catherine watched a gentle and hopeful smile stretch across Sabina's kind face. The knight softened as she looked at the noblewoman, remembering that same concerned and motherly expression often gracing her own mother's face.

Sighing, she decided it was time to voice what she'd been keeping to herself for years. 'Part of the reason why I'm so against marrying is I don't like men. I never have. When flirting with men or kissing them came up in conversation with other girls growing up, I felt left out. No matter how wonderful they

251

made it seem, I could never picture myself liking it. I found my gaze drifting towards other women, and well, I started feeling the same breathless panic I heard the others talking about when they looked at the man they fancied.'

Sabina hummed with a new found understanding. 'I see,' she replied.

The knight's shoulders dropped as she sighed with relief. 'I care for the people, of course I do. But I don't want to be tethered to a person I could never love. Given that said person would inherit Birkstead from father when he passes, I can't guarantee they'd let me handle overseeing the village, let alone even help them do so. I would be trapped in a loveless marriage, pretending that I didn't resent my spouse, and be potentially unable to distract myself from that with the welfare of the people. I also want to learn more about mother's research but I doubt they'd want me to pursue that. I know it's selfish to say, but I can't live like that.'

'That's not as selfish as you think it is. Would it be presumptuous to assume that you feel this way because you're in love already? That you're in love with that redheaded mercenary Aldric works with?'

The knight's cheeks blossomed rose red as she realised that Sabina already had an idea of what she was grappling with. Catherine awkwardly looked left and right, knowing they were alone but wanting to confirm it out of habit.

'You know about Helena?'

Sabina rolled her eyes and chuckled with amusement. 'Aldric tells me everything.'

'You know-'

A Knight's Blood

'That she's a vampire? I know,' Sabina confirming, nodding as she spoke.

Catherine pursed her lips. 'I don't know of I'm in love, but I have feelings for her. Strong ones too. At first, I was in denial because the first woman I found myself completely enchanted with was a vampire. That became less of a problem as I got to know her. There are vampires who are monsters, but I don't think Helena is one.'

Sabina patted Catherine's hand again, smiling a little wider as tears welled in her own eyes.

'As you know, Walter, Aldric and I knew your mother quite well. We never said it to anyone but her, but we agreed that the vampires who hunted other vampires were the best way to protect the population as a whole. The Church violently disagreed, but would I be wrong in assuming you've found yourself agreeing with your mother's findings?' the noblewoman asked.

'I do. Like mother, like daughter I guess,' Catherine replied, smiling sadly. 'Despite my change of mind, I wouldn't have survived if I'd fought Erik without Helena by my side. I doubt he would've been defeated if I had two other knights with me instead of her. The Church are too stubborn to admit that we humans aren't as powerful as we believe.'

'You're right,' Sabina said with another chuckle. 'Don't let anyone else hear you say that, though. It could spell trouble.'

Sabina's joke echoed Walter's warning the night he died. Well, died the first time.

The smile that touched her lips faded.

Now that she knew what truly happened to her mother, Walter's words began to make more sense. If her father had been telling the truth about the Church wanting to kill Catherine too, then there was a chance they were waiting for any excuse to come back and do so. No matter how small that chance was, Catherine knew she'd likely be looking over her shoulder for the rest of her life.

Chills ran down her spine as that realisation dawned on her.

'I know. They'll kill me like they did mother,' Catherine replied. She frowned and reached for her shift's collar, stroking her sternum where the cross would've sat. 'Walter indirectly warned me that may be the case.'

'He was a smart man.'

'Indeed.'

The two sat in silence, remembering what it was like to have the older knight around. They didn't have to say it aloud, it was clear that everything changed after both of his deaths.

Catherine closed her eyes and breathed in through her nose, letting a few tears roll freely down her face. No matter how she pretended she could handle whatever came her way on her own, she missed Walter and his gentle reassurance.

Catherine couldn't help but to wonder if Walter would've lived if she and Helena had agreed to team up that night. Helena was a formidable opponent, and even she struggled against Erik on her own. If the two of them could take Erik down, how much easier would that fight have been if another vampire had been by Helena's side? What if another, much older and stronger, vampire showed up in Birkstead next? How would she stand a chance against them even with Helena fighting beside her?

A Knight's Blood

She opened her eyes and relaxed against her pillows, ruminating on the questions that ran rampant through her thoughts. Helena's story about her life prior to meeting Erik bled into her thoughts.

Never in a million years had she thought becoming a vampire would solve her problems, and yet it presented itself as a tempting solution. She could avoid this marriage by faking her death and protect the village with her newfound undead abilities. And she could spend more time with Helena in the process.

Sabina tilted her head to the side, staring at Catherine with concern. 'Something on your mind?'

Catherine was pulled away from her thoughts as Sabina's voice captured her attention. She folded her hands on her lap and weakly smiled at the noblewoman.

'I can't help but to wonder if I could somehow protect Birkstead without sacrificing my happiness and autonomy,' she replied. 'No one expected vampires to show up and cause havoc in a village as small as ours and that's exactly what happened. Maybe Birkstead needs more than one vampire to protect it?'

Sabina stared at Catherine in stunned silence. She pursed her lips and narrowed her eyes at the knight, searching her bruised face for signs that she was joking. Upon finding none, she snorted and shook her head at Catherine's question.

'Cat, there's no need! We don't foresee another vampire like Erik to appear in England anytime soon. If we need another vampire, we'll ask Helena for her recommendations,' Sabina said, smiling and rolling her eyes at Catherine's question. 'She's been working as a vampiric mercenary for a while, she must have met some trustworthy peers during her journey.'

The knight's chest deflated as she sighed with

disappointment. Catherine didn't expect Sabina to agree with her, but the immediate and complete dismissal of her idea took her by surprise. Sabina's response stung more than she expected it to.

Sabina patted Catherine's hands, still smiling sweetly at her. 'Don't worry about that. I think pain is making you think in ridiculous ways. You're going to get through this and you'll be the leader Birkstead requires, regardless of whether you have to fight for your place for it or not. Aldric and I believe in you. Your fellow knights do too. There's more of them that support you than you realise.'

Catherine clenched her teeth as she smiled and nodded, ignoring the tears that began slipping down her cheek again. For the second time that day, betrayal sat in her throat and hindered her ability to swallow. Nausea surged and fell back down to her belly. What seemed like her only option had been dashed by Sabina's kind rationale.

'Thank you,' Catherine said. 'Your votes of confidence will help.'

Though she hated lying to Sabina and her husband, the knight couldn't voice how much her dismissive words hurt.

Catherine remained still, keeping her false smile upon her face.

Sabina let go of Catherine's hand and got up from the bed. Sabina, as always, remained a vision of the picture-perfect noblewoman. She stepped forward and held her hands in front of her body, standing tall and smiling as if the room was full of acquaintances staring at her every move.

'Rest up. I believe you'll need your strength sooner than

we all thought,' Sabina said.

Without saying anything else, Sabina left Catherine's room and closed the door behind her.

The knight waited a few moments before she let her already failing façade crack. Her body ached from drawing shallow breaths. Catherine's red and puffy eyes prickled. Her drying tears refused to stop falling. Her thoughts spiralled into darkness. Hope slipped from her grasp the longer she sat against her pillows.

She needed to talk to Helena and she needed to do it soon.

23

Catherine battled with her sorrow in near silence during the hours after her conversations with her father and Sabina. Her eyes fluttered closed. The weight of her fatigue forced her eyelids to remain shut. Catherine found brief relief in the darkness. No matter how desperately she wished to sleep, the nothingness she previously welcomed was immediately flooded. Thousands of thoughts shouted over each other, fighting to command the tired knight's attention.

Her fireplace crackled and spat. The wood that fuelled the fire became nothing more than char and ash. Flames burnt the pinch of dried lavender that was thrown into the hearth, dispersing the fragrance throughout the room.

She drew in a sharp breath as something soft brushed the underside of her jaw, leaving tingles dancing along her skin in its wake. A smile touched her lips as a familiar voice reached her ears.

'Have you managed to get any rest?'

Catherine forced her eyes open and saw Helena standing beside her bed. Seeing Helena's beautiful face brightened the darkness that hung over her.

'No,' Catherine replied with a tired sigh. 'I'm in too much pain to get comfortable and my mind won't stop racing.'

Helena looked down adoringly at Catherine, sweetly

exposing her fangs as she smiled at the knight.

'The healers might have something that can help with that. Do you want some tonic? Perhaps some soup?' Helena offered.

Catherine slowly shook her head. 'No thanks. I'm not hungry.'

'Well, I do have something that might cheer you up,' the vampire said, her voice wavering as if she were singing a child's tune.

The knight raised an eyebrow at Helena's cheery response. 'Oh?'

Helena pulled a square of cotton out of her pocket and carefully placed it upon Catherine's lap, ensuring she touched the fabric's sides and nothing else. Despite the fact she handled it as if she'd burn herself with foul-smelling water if she touched the centre, Helena grinned with excitement.

Catherine took the fabric parcel into her hands and pulled the cotton layer away, revealing what lay inside.

Her mother's necklace.

Delight chased away some of the fear, anger, and sorrow that coloured her thoughts.

The silver cross chilled the tips of Catherine's fingers as she brushed its familiar surface once more.

'How did you find it?' the knight asked, her mouth falling open with relief.

'Aldric found it while he was in Birkstead earlier,'

Helena explained. 'Your peers have been skittish after vampires caused mayhem so close to home. Thankfully, Erik doesn't pose a threat anymore, but Aldric had to go down there to ensure the younger knights felt safe during their rounds. He found it when he was inspecting the scene of the battle and wanted you to have your necklace sooner rather than later.'

'Thank you. I appreciate the both of you and everything you've done for me.'

Helena tenderly kissed Catherine's forehead.

Catherine looked up at Helena. Her heart fluttered when she saw her fanged smile. Though the vampire couldn't stand in sunshine without her skin blistering, Helena's smile emanated its warmth.

The knight looked at the vampire, her chest aching over the information she'd learnt hours before. Catherine couldn't keep the news from Helena. She needed to know what storm was about to break over what remained of Catherine's life.

'My father informed me that I am to be married,' Catherine said, her voice breaking. 'To a nobleman from France.'

The vampire's smile fell. She cradled the knight's face. Helena tenderly brushed her thumb across Catherine's cheek. She saw the desperation and devastation in Catherine's eyes and bit back the urge to fold her into her arms. Instead, she pressed another kiss to the knight's forehead to avoid hurting Catherine further.

A small smile touched Catherine's lips. Her heart melted as the vampire showered her in soft caresses.

'His timing is rather cruel,' Helena commented bitterly. 'What about getting those two sets of remains? Don't they change anything? Did he even ask how you were before he told you?'

The knight sighed. Disappointment returned and hatred bubbled up along with it.

'My father doesn't care about anything that cannot secure his position or elevate it. He's excited for me to marry the third cousin to the Dauphiné,' Catherine replied. 'He doesn't care that I'm going to lose everything I worked to achieve. It didn't matter what I did, if he wanted something, he was going to do whatever he could to get it. He's always been selfish like that.'

Helena looked into Catherine's eyes and saw the sorrow and fear that the knight tried so hard to hide.

'Oh Catherine, I'm so sorry,' Helena said.

'I should've known better. Whether I completed the quest or not, my father would've set up the marriage without any consideration for me. He's not known for honesty or compassion,' Catherine replied, holding back tears once more. 'Aldric thinks he became that way after losing mother, but I think he was like that even before then.'

The vampire stretched out beside her on her bed, nestling her head into the crook of Catherine's neck. She peppered the underside of Catherine's jaw with tiny kisses, eager to cheer her up despite the strong stench of the poultices slathered over the knight's skin. She threaded her fingers in-between Catherine's and held them close to her chest.

'I wish there was something I could do,' Helena said. The vampire remained silent for a few moments. A toothy grin spread across her lips as a thought popped into her head. 'I could kill your father and the prospective groom.'

Though Helena's idea was tempting, Catherine shook

her head.

'Well, vampires have glamour abilities. Why don't I charm him into changing his mind? He fell for Erik's tricks. He'd fall for mine too,' Helena offered.

Catherine snorted. 'It could work, but he's so excited to join the French court through marriage that I doubt even magic could change his mind.'

Silence drifted over the two as thoughts swam in their minds, each searching for a way to get Catherine out of marrying the French noble her father had picked for her.

Her vow to make her father's life Hell echoed with violent glee. If there was ever an appropriate time to pitch the idea Sabina dismissed to Helena, this was it.

'You might not be able to change his mind, but you could change me.'

Helena stared at Catherine in shock. 'You want to re-awaken as a vampire?'

'Yes.'

The vampire watched Catherine carefully, examining her expression for uncertainty.

Catherine's expression didn't falter, not even for a moment.

'Are you certain about this? I cannot prepare you for everything that is to come. It won't matter if I tell you that the process was the most painful change my body has gone through, you're only going to compare that statement to how you feel now. It's a very different pain to healing from open wounds and

262

excessive bruising,' Helena began to explain, keeping her tone as even as possible.

Catherine looked Helena in her beautiful red eyes and nodded.

'I couldn't be more certain. Though it began as a rouge thought, I couldn't stop thinking about it. The more I thought about it, the more it became my best option.'

Helena raised an eyebrow at that statement. She was suspicious, but the vampire didn't immediately shut her idea down like Sabina had.

'Go on,' Helena said. 'How is it your best option?'

Hope bloomed upon her lips so widely the corners of Catherine's mouth threatened to crack open.

'At first, I considered killing my father but I don't believe that would change anything. I never considered killing the man he chose, that would cause more problems than it solved. While this nobleman might never be crowned, he's still somewhere in the French line of succession. There's a risk of starting a war with France if he died or was injured. Forget just Birkstead, that wouldn't be good for England.'

'I hadn't even considered that,' Helena chirped with a playful hum.

Catherine rolled her eyes. 'I think you would have considered it down the line or there'd be a lot more vampires orchestrating wars just to soothe their bloodthirst and boost their egos.'

'You're right,' she said. 'Maybe vampire politics

Gwendolyn K. Blackthorne

wouldn't be too foreign to you after all.' Helena's cheeky grin
faded, clearing her throat for the dramatics. 'Now, tell me the ac-
tual reason why you think becoming a vampire is your only option. When we first met you thought all vampires were monsters,
and now you wish to become one. What changed your mind?'

Catherine clutched the cross in her palm, savouring how
the silver's chill seeped through the cotton as if it were nothing but water. She breathed in through her nose and out of her
mouth, preparing to make her case to the vampire beside her.

'There's a big chance I might have to hang up my sword
and relinquish my duties when I'm married. I won't let that happen. I intend for that not to happen. I swore I'd protect the people
and I don't care if doing so comes with a title or not. We killed
Erik, that much is certain. But I couldn't help but to wonder what
would happen if another, more powerful, vampire showed up and
we couldn't defeat them. What would become of the people?'

'I understand, but there has to be more to it than that.'

'We survived, but I don't wish to take chances going
forward. Two vampires are much more efficient than one. Your
time in Athens proves that, right? The coven of vampire hunters
you worked with?'

Helena pursed her lips. 'It does.'

'With two vampires protecting Birkstead, the knights
won't be so skittish. The people will sleep better knowing they're
safe. Aldric could commission a vampire that came with your
recommendations, but what if you had a partner who was trained
by you? There would be no surprises regarding abilities or views
and you'd know where the both of you stood.'

'Well–'

A Knight's Blood

Catherine thought she'd cried all her tears earlier, yet more settled in the corner of her eyes. Her chest ached. Her lungs struggled to properly inflate. She had to say what really weighed on her mind or admit she'd rather die than follow her father's orders.

'I can't marry a man,' the knight blurted, her voice wavering like the tears upon her lashes. 'What life is one lived without love? Without affection? Dooming myself to an existence of resentment and disgust towards a man is bad enough. Being an unwilling vessel for his spawn would destroy me.'

'Cat–'

The heartbreak in Helena's gaze forced Catherine's trembling tears to trickle down her cheeks. Her ribs felt as if they could pop her lungs if she held her breath too long. As her eyes continued to water, her eyelids itched. Everything hurt. The knight couldn't stop herself.

'I hope to God you aren't going to tell me that marriage isn't as bad as I think it is. Sabina already gave me that line and it didn't ease my worries. Men have never piqued my interest and the idea of being intimate with one disgusts me.'

Helena ran her thumb across Catherine's tear-slickened cheek, smiling sadly at the knight baring her heart. 'I would never say that. I care too much about you to repeat the lies mother and father used to tell me in my time as a mortal.'

Catherine returned the smile, leaning into Helena's touch once more. The vampire's touch eased the ache in her chest.

'I am unsure if what I feel towards you is love, but I won't deny that I care deeply for you too. Part of the reason I even considered reawakening in the first place was to spend more time with you. There was no way I'd want to pine over you as I faked being happily married to someone I couldn't care about. I don't want the time we have to just be stolen kisses in the darkness. I don't want our happiness or my desire for Birkstead's protection to be hindered by anyone's expectations of me or you. Helena, I want to protect Birkstead with you. As your lover.'

That joyous warmth Catherine noticed before returned. The crows' feet on either side of Helena's face deepened. The vampire practically radiated happiness.

Helena nodded, her fangs touching her bottom lip as her smile widened. 'I would love nothing more. But what about your mother's research? What happens to it if the reawakening fails?'

'It won't,' Catherine replied, her response strong. 'I have faith in myself and I have faith in you. If it does come to that, I would want nobody else but you to search for it and keep it safe.'

The vampire nodded once more, silently agreeing to do so should the worst happen. 'Very well. You've convinced me.'

Relief surged through Catherine's mind so fast she couldn't help but to laugh victoriously. She pressed her lips to Helena's nose, excited that someone finally understood her wants and needs.

'Would you like me to try and reawaken you now?' Helena asked.

'Yes,' the knight replied, letting what she hoped was the last of her tears roll down her cheek.

The vampire cupped the other woman's face, ensuring that her blue eyes were looking into her own red ones. 'I want to remind you that reawakening is a painful process. There will be no promises that any humans will not be harmed when you're adjusting to the change. Can you live with potentially killing someone to let your body adjust to the new magic?'

'I'm not afraid. I've killed before, it's not foreign to me. That is a potential I must recognise and accept,' Catherine affirmed, holding herself as confidently as her aching body would allow.

'I'll be here when you close your eyes. And I'll be here when you reawaken.'

'I look forward to it.'

After Catherine spoke those words, Helena helped her get comfortable against the mattress. She placed the fabric still containing the cross onto the table beside Catherine's bed for safekeeping.

The vampire straddled the knight's hips, smiling down at her. Helena's hair slid over her shoulders, hanging by her cheek like a curtain of molten copper. She leant forward and pressed her lips against Catherine's in a chaste kiss, pulling away to kiss the knight's neck.

Catherine's heart thrummed in her chest as the vampire's lips touched her flesh. Anticipation raced down her spine. Her neck prickled when Helena pressed pretty little kisses against her skin. A sigh fell from her lips as the vampire nipped the sensitive area she planned to bite.

'Do it,' she breathed. 'Please.'

The vampire smiled against Catherine's neck. Helena pressed her hand against the knight's shoulder to keep her steady against the bed.

Catherine cried out as Helena's fangs punctured her

neck. Pain and pleasure shocked her system as blood welled in the newly opened wound. She grasped the vampire's waist, holding her tight as she felt herself begin to fade.

Helena drank greedily, desperate not to let a single drop escape. Despite her reluctance to stop, she pulled away from Catherine's neck and watched the knight's eyes flutter shut. She ripped her bottom lip open with a fang and kissed Catherine, ensuring her own blood flowed into the knight's mouth and down her throat.

Catherine's grip on Helena's waist weakened. Just feeling Helena's weight upon her hips was enough to chase away any fear that the vampire wasn't going to reawaken her at all. Her mind wavered as blood seeped from her body. The last thing she tasted was copper.

Thoughts of Helena were the last to take centre stage before she slipped into unconsciousness and death's cold embrace.

Catherine and Helena's story concludes in *A Knight's Duty*

Acknowledgements

Writing is stereotypically seen as a solitary art. Like most stereotypes, that's far from the truth. The reality is more complex than that. Storytelling of any form is collaborative. It's easier to push past the doubt that nibbles your mind when you have someone to bounce ideas off or reassure you when needed.

It's taken me a long time to learn how to ask for help and realize that I am not less than because I needed support; everyone needs it from time to time. There is no shame in realizing that. A Knight's Blood wouldn't exist in your hands or on your device if it weren't for those who supported me through the entire process.

Jay, I cannot thank you enough for your hard work editing this novel. You were the first person to read A Knight's Blood after I was unsure how to improve it further. I cannot properly express how much it means to have your feedback.

Blue and Emma, thank you both so much for listening to my rantings and uncertainties about this book. Your encouragement means more than you could ever know.

I want to thank Sarah from The Illustrated Page Book Design for creating this gorgeous cover and bringing my vision to life.

I want to thank my husband William for being my rock during a rough period of personal healing and a pandemic. Never before have I had someone love me so unconditionally and deeply as you. I will always be grateful for your love and support.

And last but not least, I wish to thank you, the reader, for picking up my book and deciding to give it a go. I hope you had as much fun reading A Knight's Blood as I had writing it. It's such an exciting thing to publish a novel and it means so much to me that you decided to read my debut.

Here's to many more novels to come!

About the Author

Gwendolyn K. Blackthorne is an Australian paranormal romance author living in Melbourne with her loving partner. Her lifelong curiosity with vampires and the occult proves to be an everlasting source of wonder and ideas.

She has a Bachelor of Arts (Professional and Creative Writing) from Deakin University and has always been an avid reader and storyteller. When she's not reading and writing, Gwendolyn enjoys baking sweets, and indulging in various crafts such as sewing garments, cross-stitch, and doll customization.

A Knight's Blood is her debut novel.